"Are you following me?"

Nina turned to see Jacob, shoes in hand, stepping into the shallow surf beside her.

"Hello, again," he said. "I did see you coming this way, yes." He gave her a smile. "I've always loved the ocean. It's a great place to think."

She fought back a frown. So, he hadn't exactly come with a desire to spend time with her. Why had she secretly hoped he had?

"You must have quite a lot to think about."

"Yes. My enlistment is almost up. I've already extended it once, on account of the disaster."

Nina's heart fell. What would she do if he were to leave?

Not that they could be anything more than friends.

Cynthia Hickey is the author of six historical romances with Love Inspired Heartsong Presents, as well as several cozy mysteries and novellas with Barbour Publishing. She is active on Facebook, Twitter and Goodreads. Cynthia lives in Arizona with her husband, one of their seven children, two dogs and two cats. She has five grandchildren who tell everyone they know that "Nana is a writer." Visit her website at cynthiahickey.com.

Books by Cynthia Hickey

Love Inspired Heartsong Presents

CYNTHIA HICKEY

The Soldier's Redemption

HEARTSONG
PRESENTS

Recycling programs
for this product may
not exist in your area.

LOVE INSPIRED BOOKS

ISBN-13: 978-0-373-48775-2

The Soldier's Redemption

www.Harlequin.com

Printed in U.S.A.

May the Lord answer you in the day of trouble;
May the name of the God of Jacob defend you.
—*Psalms* 20:1

To all the survivors, today and yesterday

Chapter 1

San Francisco, April 18, 1906

Nina Hansen fastened the last button on her dress and slipped her feet into her shoes. Smiling, she glanced out her bedroom window. Just as a flock of pigeons took off from the roof of the building. One smacked into the windowpane, inches away from her nose.

She jumped back, gasping, and clutched the high neckline of her dress. She laughed at her unaccustomed jitters. A dog barked from down the road, piercing the eerie silence of the Maria Kip Orphanage. The hair on Nina's arms stood at attention, prickling her skin. The morning waited as if holding its breath.

Shaking her head at her foolishness, Nina slipped her feet into slippers. Her nerves were raw, her body tired. Last night, two of the teenage boys apparently didn't understand the rule of lights out. She still needed to take them to task about keeping the younger children awake by casting hand puppet shadows on the wall.

She chalked off her uneasy feeling to the past three days of unseasonably warm weather. Already a faint sheen of perspiration dotted her upper lip. With a sigh, she took a step toward the door.

The earth groaned. The floor bucked under her. Grasping the bedpost, she fought to keep her footing while her gaze locked on the clock, which read 5:13 a.m. She counted seconds, focusing on her heartbeat and breathing. Earthquakes weren't uncommon in California and often stopped within seconds. There was no need for alarm.

Her wood-framed mirror crashed to the floor, littering the polished planks with shards of glass. Her prized camera swung from a hook on the wall like the pendulum of a clock. The drawers of her dresser bounced open. A crack the width of her hand split the wall. This was no ordinary earthquake.

Plaster rained down, coating her hair and shoulders with powdered flecks. Nausea rose in her stomach, just as it did when she rode the ferry. The trembling eased, then commenced with a vengeance. Her wrought-iron bed bounced away from the wall.

From the other rooms, screams and cries rent the air. The children!

How would only two women get all one hundred and twenty-five of them to safety when the floor heaved beneath their feet like a horse unaccustomed to a saddle? The movement was short and choppy like the waves of the sea, crisscrossed by a tide as mighty as a tsunami. *God, help them.*

Nina dashed for the door with the grace of a drunken sailor. She clutched the doorjamb, using its frame as protection, and kept her eyes glued on the second hand of the clock. Anything to take her mind away from the roaring around her. A sound like waves crashing against the cliffs filled her head with its pounding.

In the hall, Mrs. Fox, the superintendent, rushed from room to room, restoring order and issuing directions. The only clue to the woman's panic was her pale face and her hair, which was slapped sloppily into a bun. "To the yard, children. Grab your clothes and hurry, please. Older ones help the younger ones get outside." Her efficient, clipped manner soothed Nina's frazzled nerves and brought her to her senses.

This wasn't the first earthquake she'd endured. She needed to help. The children needed rescuing.

She abandoned her place of safety under the door's frame, wishing the other employees of the orphanage didn't have nights off. Of course a disaster of this magnitude would happen when there were only two adults supervising.

A horrific rumble roared from the front of the building as she ran down the hall. She glanced over her shoulder as the front end of the building collapsed into the street. A cloud of dust plumed, obscuring her vision and clogging her throat. She choked back a scream as the chimney followed, raining red brick across the lawn.

They were going to die.

Forty-five seconds later, to the best of Nina's counting, the shaking stopped. She wiped tears from her face as the children's screams turned to wails. Nina scooped a toddler into her arms, then followed the orphans as they banged down the stairs and rushed outside.

Tears smeared Mrs. Fox's white-dusted face, and she lifted clasped hands toward heaven. "All accounted for, praise God."

Sobs blocked Nina's throat. They were lucky. She laid a kiss on the child she held, then passed the little girl off to an older child. "No injuries?"

"A few bumps from falling plaster, nothing serious. God is with us." Mrs. Fox clapped her hands. "Gather around, children." Like a flock of baby chicks, they crowded close, dirty faces turned in her direction. "We must give thanks to God for His protection."

From the corner of her eye, Nina noticed two teenage boys skulking to the back of the building. What were the rascals up to now? She followed. "Johnny?"

The tallest one shook his head, grabbed a dangling water pipe, and swung upward, scrabbling with the skill of a monkey to the second floor. His companion, towheaded Daniel, quickly followed suit. Within seconds, quilts, cots and personal treasures hit the ground, littering the once beautiful flower garden.

"Come down this instant!" Nina planted her fists on her hips. "The building isn't safe." Her heart lodged in her throat. Any moment now the floor would give way and they'd be lost.

Johnny stuck his head out the window. "Not until I get my little brother some pants. He can't roam around the city in a nightgown."

"Please, hurry." Nina bit her lip as the house creaked and groaned. Surely, it would fall on their heads.

Clutching a pair of brown woolen britches in one hand, Johnny shimmied down the pipe, Daniel in close pursuit.

When they hit the ground, Nina grabbed them each by an arm. "What possessed you to do something so dangerous? You scared the wits out of me."

"More than the earthquake?" A dimple winked in Johnny's cheek. "I had to get Sam's pants, Miss Hansen. He looks like a girl in his nightgown." He pulled her camera from beneath his oversize shirt and presented it to her with a grin. "I also thought you might want this."

Nina grabbed him close and ruffled his hair. He'd thought not only of his brother, but of her. Fresh tears stung the backs of her eyes. How could she stay mad at such a fearless softhearted young man? The fifteen-year-old was old enough to be on his own, making a living any way he could in San Francisco, but no one had the heart to send him away, despite his tendency to break rules.

"Thank you." She hung her camera around her neck. "This means a lot to me."

His grin faded. "I saw smoke rising south of Market Street. You can see quite a ways from the second floor."

Panic spasmed in her chest. "Fires?"

"Yes, ma'am. Looks like spot fires dotted all over San Francisco. They'll be spreading fast." He whirled and dashed to his younger brother's side.

Nina approached Mrs. Fox. "Did you hear?"

The woman cast a nervous glance down the street. "Yes. We need to get the children to the ferry. We'll take them to Ross Valley over in Marin County."

The ground shuddered under her. Nina grabbed Mrs. Fox's arm. Another wall crumbled and clattered to the ground. A second earthquake?

Nina's blood ran cold. "I think the sooner the better."

In single file, with Mrs. Fox in the front and Nina behind, they and the children set out into the heart of San Francisco. Buildings leaned against each other, knocked off their foundations, like people who had drunk too much. Geysers gushed from broken water mains, flooding the streets. Nina forced back the bile rising in her throat and clutched the hand of the nearest child. They'd be all right. God wouldn't let them survive the quake to allow harm to come to them now.

Sergeant Jacob Taft took a deep breath of salty sea air and shook off the lingering effects of the earthquake. He should've gone straight to Fort Mason, but couldn't deny his morning ritual of watching the sun rise over the Pacific. The beach always soothed him. The fearsome lapping of the waves slowly subsided.

He was days away from being a civilian again. Now he suspected his enlistment would be extended.

Footsteps pounded behind him. Jacob stood at attention, awaiting orders, the morning's calm as destroyed as the city behind him.

"Permission to speak, sir!"

Without turning, Jacob nodded. "Granted." He'd known as soon as the earthquake hit that his furlough was over.

"General Funston has ordered the First Battalion to move into the city to guard federal property and assist the local police in keeping order, sir!"

Jacob turned to address the sergeant beside him. "How did you know where to find me?"

"You are here every morning, sir. Furlough or not."

Jacob shrugged. His habits were no secret. "What about the fort?" With the fires dotting the landscape, Fort Mason would be in danger, as well.

"A small contingent of men will stay behind. General Funston is setting up a refugee camp at the Golden Gate Park and another at the Presidio. He requested you be at the Golden Gate camp by sundown to establish order."

"What about the fires? We can help fight them." He clenched his fists, stuffing his fear of fires into the deepest part of him. Now was not the time to succumb to matters of his own.

"He said nothing in regards to fighting fires, sir." The man saluted.

Jacob nodded and waited until the sergeant retreated before releasing a sigh. In charge of a refugee camp? He shuddered and headed to his barracks. He was the last person to be responsible for a multitude of hurting people. He'd failed to keep his family of three safe. How could he watch over thousands?

After pulling a rucksack from his locker, Jacob tossed in a change of uniform and an ammunition box. He grabbed his rifle, fastened the bayonet, then marched outside and joined the First Battalion of Army Engineers.

Captain Walker paced, hands clasped behind his back. "The fire department is unequipped to deal with the fires breaking out. Gas pipes have burst and water mains ruptured. The fire is rapidly engulfing the city. Panic and looting will be rampant. Men, report to chief of police at the Hall of Justice. He will give you further orders. Commence."

What about General Funston's orders? Jacob took his place at the front of the line and led the men into the city, torn between orders to keep the peace and the need to help stop the fires from engulfing the city.

He marched down Van Ness Avenue, past Saint Mary's Cathedral, heading toward a thousand-foot plume of smoke rising above the city's buildings. Within hours, the smaller fires would converge and become one raging inferno, devouring everything in its path.

He forced his heart to remain impassive, keeping his eyes forward, not focusing on the streams of people flooding the streets, or the wounded and dying lying in the gutters and under the debris. Orders were orders. The acrid smell of dust from the rubble and burned wood stung his nostrils. He increased the pace. Once they received orders to do so, then, and only then, could they stop and help those they were sent to aid.

By 7 a.m., amidst rousing cheers from a crowd happy to see them, they stood while Chief of Police Duke relayed his plan of action. "Two men per block will patrol the streets. Shoot any person caught looting or committing any serious misdemeanor. No cooking inside of dwellings. Order people to cook in the street. We cannot take the chance of more fires. Not until each home is checked for gas leaks. Some of you have been issued instructions to man refugee camps. Others are ordered to remain in the city. If you have not received a direct order, then use your judgment where you are needed most. The spread of fire is our biggest concern. Use force, if necessary, to convince the civilians to help." The man squared his shoulders. "General Funston has agreed we are to use you in any way we see fit. Fighting fires and maintaining control is where I see the greatest need. Dismissed and may God go with you."

"I heard they let the prisoners go," a man in the crowd reported. "With only the worst cases being sent to San Quentin."

"A body isn't safe on the streets," a woman cried. "Thank goodness the army is here to protect us."

Jacob didn't know how a few hundred men against hundreds of thousands of civilians could warrant protection around the clock, but he'd do his best. He accepted a paper thrust into his hands, then made his way to the steps of the Hall. Keeping his face impassive, he read aloud, "Refugee camps will be set up at the Presidio and Golden Gate Park. The Salvationists have several stations throughout the city where you can obtain food and water. Please do not loiter in the city."

While cries of outrage filled the air, he made his way back to the street and began assigning blocks for his men to patrol. He took the block around the government buildings, and snagged two men. "Clear these structures of all documents and transport them to the base. Recruit civilians to help if need be. Everyone pitches in. If they don't want to help, order them to the camps."

"Yes, sir!" The private saluted and dashed off.

Jacob shook his head at the futility of it all. Guarding walls of wood and stone while injured people lined the streets. He had joined the army to protect, not patrol streets full of people refusing to leave after a disaster of this earthquake's magnitude.

"To the camps!" he ordered the nonmilitary onlookers. "If not, start clearing the streets of brick and debris." A group of men stepped forward. "We'll help."

Then one by one, or in pairs, other men stepped forward offering their services.

Jacob nodded, doing his best to keep his emotions from showing on his face, while his heart marveled at the men's willingness to help. Surely, they had lost everything in the quake. "And your help will be greatly appreciated. We need the streets cleared. Any opposition, let one of my men know."

Two women, escorting a long line of children in assorted articles of clothing, passed by. The tall, willowy, strawberry-blonde woman glanced Jacob's way. Shadowed blue eyes peered from a face covered in dirt. Still, she was beautiful. Their gazes locked. She nodded in his direction and steered a young boy back into place.

Jacob's shoulders slumped. Orphans left without a home like so many other San Franciscans.

The ground rumbled under his feet, like a giant beast complaining of hunger pangs. Mortar and plaster fell from the remaining buildings, increasing the danger to the milling citizens. The blonde fell to her knees, and Jacob darted forward, folding his body over her and the boy she guarded. To the woman's credit, she didn't scream as an aftershock toppled most of the still-standing structures.

Jacob held the woman tighter, catching a whiff of lavender and vanilla over the odor of dust. He couldn't help but notice how right she felt in his arms, as if she were made to be there. He shook off the notion and glanced

up as a chimney fell, crushing two of the men who'd
volunteered just moments before. Poor souls. It wasn't
a fitting end to men who had only wanted to help. Dust
coated the people around them and caked Jacob's eyes.
A fierce roaring filled his ears, along with the screams of
the children. He wanted to cover them all, protect them
from this hell. At least one child and a brave woman was
better than none.

Something smacked his shoulder with a bone-jarring
thud. Jacob grunted against the impact. Nothing felt broken, but he knew he'd sport a multitude of bruises for a
few days.

Seconds later, the aftershock stopped, and Jacob
stood to his feet and surveyed his surroundings. People
emerged from doorways where they'd taken shelter. Others uncurled themselves from where they'd dropped in
the street. Just a fraction of the number of people Jacob
would be responsible for, and he'd already failed to save
a couple of them. But he could find a way to help the two
in front of him.

He assisted the woman and child to their feet. "Are you
all right?"

"Yes, thanks to you." She motioned her chin toward the
bay. "We're trying to get the children to the ferry."

Even though she was covered in a fine dust, Jacob could
see her beauty. Eyes the color of a summer sky, hair like
shimmering strands of silk. She reached his chin, tall for
a woman, and held herself with the regality of a queen,
despite the rip in her navy wool skirt and stains on her
white blouse. A camera hung around her neck, partially
obscured by long sections of hair that fell free of a bun
at her nape. He'd like to know her better, under different
circumstances. It wasn't every day a man met a woman
who faced tragedy without screams or tears. But, now

was not the time for fanciful ideas. He had work to do, and plenty of it.

"Let me find someone to help you." Jacob called for one of his men to escort the large group, then tipped his hat. "Good day, ma'am. Godspeed."

Chapter 2

Nina watched the soldier march away, a strong, muscular figure in tan service breeches, single-breasted sack coat and russet leather boots. A hero. A man who didn't think twice about putting his body in the way of falling debris to protect a stranger.

A hand touched her shoulder. "Miss Hansen, we must continue." Mrs. Fox motioned them forward to where another soldier led the way. "If we tarry, we linger in harm's way."

Throngs of people traveled in the same direction. One lady carried a birdcage full of kittens while her parrot rode on her shoulder, singing a ditty. A man pushed a wheelbarrow filled with books.

Nina's fingers itched to snap photographs of the devastation and human nature around her. An elderly man, tenderly clutching a pot of calla lilies, shuffled by, muttering to himself, while a scrub woman, holding a broom in one hand and a large black hat adorned with ostrich plumes in the other, tottered on high heels. Another woman wore a fox stole over a flannel nightgown. Oh, the sights Nina could record if she only had film.

They passed a mercantile where the owner, wearing a white apron over his suit, swept the front stoop. Debris crunched under their feet, biting through Nina's thin slippers. She glanced at the fire gaining ground behind them. Already her nostrils stung from the smoke. The storekeeper swept in vain. Soon, his shop would be like so many others, nothing but ashes and brick.

By the time they reached the bay, Nina's feet ached. She wished she could've changed into her work shoes. A glance at a barefoot child, and guilt stabbed her. She musn't complain when others had less now than she did.

The soldier assigned to them hurried to the ferryman. Within moments, he returned. "He will take you now, before too many folks need his services."

Mrs. Fox shook the hand of the young man assigned to help them. "Thank you for accompanying us."

With a nod, he dashed off.

Nina longed to join him. How much good she could do. The pictures she could capture to let the world know what had happened. She moved to follow the soldier, hesitated and turned back to Mrs. Fox. "I must stay behind."

Mrs. Fox's face paled. "Why, dear?" Her gaze darted over the children, then landed on Nina. "The children need you. I need you."

Nina shook her head. Pain lanced her heart. "There's a city in agony. I want to photograph the calamity for posterity." Nina laid her hands on the other woman's shoulders. "I want to stay and help. I'm needed here more. Perhaps even the Salvation Army can use me."

"But, a single woman, alone in a city full of soldiers, and…"

"God will be with me." Nina straightened. "You and the children are my family. I'll find you when this is over. There will be so many people without homes, children who are lost. I can help them." She knew she could find a way to lessen the burdens of others. "I feel led to do this,

Mrs. Fox. Please, understand. You will have help where you're going. I can help here."

Mrs. Fox cupped her cheek, while tears marked her own. "Go. You're right. There are others here who need you, and we must each follow God's will for our lives. The older girls can help me keep an eye on the younger children. We will miss you."

As Mrs. Fox and her charges boarded the ferry, tears streamed down Nina's face. They had been her family since she two years old, when she'd been abandoned at the orphanage. Swiping away her tears, she headed back into the city, its buildings now covered by a haze of smoke, determined to find somewhere to serve.

She jumped over a crack in the once fine brick road, glancing down into the dark crevice. How far did it go? If she were to fall, would she disappear, never to be seen again? She tore her gaze away and focused on the mayhem around her.

Already, the streets were patrolled by police and soldiers. Orders for people to stay home or head to a refugee camp added to the calamity. Smoke billowed in white mushroom clouds over the skyline.

A fire truck clattered past, tooting its horn. Nina leaped aside. The horses pulling the red steam engine rolled their eyes in fright. The driver yelled for people to get out of the way, and a mother grabbed her daughter by the collar, yanking her to the sidewalk.

Once the engine passed, people clogged the street once more. Nina's nerves stretched to the breaking point, leaving her trembling as she maneuvered around piles of debris. A woman wailed from an alcove, her arms wrapped around the still body of a child.

Nina couldn't breathe. She leaned against a sagging building and wrapped her arms around her middle. Why hadn't she gone with Mrs. Fox to a safe place? A place where darkness and grief didn't hover over everything in sight? She wasn't strong enough to survive such terror.

"It's God's judgment!" A man dressed in a soot-covered nightshirt, bony knees showing beneath a filthy hem, staggered by, a makeshift bandage wound around his head. Crimson streaked the white cloth. "The end of the world is near! Repent! Repent!"

Nina's mind whirled. Was this the end? The Armageddon promised in the Bible?

She pushed away from the rough brick of the building. She needed to get away, buy film, start doing what she'd stayed behind to do. Disregarding her unladylike conduct, she lifted her skirts, and raced along Montgomery Street to a photo and goods shop she'd spotted earlier. Out of breath, she slowed and entered the store.

A clerk reclined in a wooden office chair behind a counter. Why was he still there? Was he not aware of the danger?

"I need film for a 3A Kodak Special." She dug in her reticule for coins. "And a pair of boots, if you have them."

The man waved his hand. "Take what you need. It's all going to burn anyway."

"Please, let me pay."

"No need. Insurance will cover the loss." He reached to a shelf and withdrew a box. He tossed it at her. "Go. Record history for all mankind."

"I intend to." She shoved the film in her pockets. "Are you all right, sir?"

He shrugged and pulled a cigar from the breast pocket of his pin-striped vest. "Considering that I'm losing everything? I'm great."

His sarcasm wasn't lost on Nina. He didn't look great. Actually, the man looked quite drunk for such an early hour. Her gaze landed on an empty amber bottle on the counter.

"Why are you still here?" She placed her hand on his. "Come with me."

"I'll leave before the fire gets here." He lit his cigar, puffed and blew a smoke ring at the ceiling. "Let me enjoy what I used to have. There are boots on the shelf in the corner, left behind by my daughter when she fled. You are welcome to them."

Nina said a prayer for his safety. "Can you direct me to the nearest Red Cross or Salvation Army? I'd like to volunteer."

"I'm sure they can use you." He rolled his cigar through his fingers. "We've been told no fires inside the buildings. Do you think they'd shoot me if they knew I lit this? There are also orders to shoot looters. Does remaining in one's own place of business count as looting?"

She opened her mouth, then closed it when no words came. The man had lost his mind.

He shrugged. "Try any of the churches. Someone will be able to direct you. Better hurry. By noon, this whole area will be nothing but ashes."

Nina nodded. "Take care, sir. And thank you for the film. And boots."

She loaded the camera and snapped a quick shot of the storekeeper, head tilted back, blowing rings into the air. Then, reaching to a high shelf, she grabbed the pair of boots, in her size thankfully, and shoved her feet into them. She left her slippers behind, then whirled and dashed outside.

The smoke had increased while she'd been in the shop. She pulled her handkerchief from her handbag to hold over her nose.

A shot rang out. A man carrying a cardboard box fell in the doorway of a drugstore. She screamed.

A soldier whirled in her direction. "No loitering!" He waved his gun at her.

With a shriek, Nina ran. What would the soldier do if he found her pockets stuffed with film? Would he think she'd stolen it? Would the storekeeper be around to back up her story? She gulped and ran until she turned onto Van Ness Avenue. Her chest heaved from trying to breathe in the smoke-filled air.

A steady stream of people headed in the direction of Golden Gate Park. One elderly lady grabbed Nina's arm. "Come with us."

Nina stepped back. "I'll be along later."

She stopped to catch her breath on Sacramento Street. The entire front wall of a house lay in the street, blocking traffic on one side. Haze hovered over the remains like thick fog in a nightmare. In front of the house, a family sat in chairs and watched the mass exodus of people stream past. Nina snapped their photograph. What a perfect picture of the day's atrocity. Devastation and shock. People determined to hold on to what they owned for as long as possible.

Another woman stood alone in front of her fallen house. "No one died. No one's here. What am I to do? Where do I look for them?"

Nina shook her head, tears stinging at the despair on the woman's face. She lowered her camera. She refused to photograph hopelessness. The day held enough sorrow without sharing too much of it with the rest of the world. She'd get on film stories of heroic bravery and people moving forward.

A broken water main filled a crater in the middle of the street. Men darted back and forth filling buckets in an effort to save the mansions lining the street. Nina, numb from the horror of it all, raised her camera again. The air heated as the fire consumed everything it touched. As the flames moved, so did the people, block by block, until even those resting on their chairs moved away.

When the crowd grew too large for Nina to shoot photos effectively, she scooted down a side street. Occasionally, she heard gunshots, and she cringed with each one. This must be what hell was like. Darkness, wailing, loss of hope.

Three soldiers peered up at the roof of a hotel. Flames licked up the sides, until only a flat portion of roof remained untouched. Two men waved frantically from the top as the fire kissed their feet.

"We'll never get them down, the poor souls," one of the soldiers said.

Another, with three stripes on his sleeve, shook his head. "We can't let them burn. Shoot them."

"No!" Nina rushed forward and pushed the soldier taking aim. "That's murder." What kind of terror had the earthquake unleashed?

"Are you crazy, lady?" The man shoved her away, knocking her to the ground. "They don't deserve to burn alive." He took aim. "We're doing them a favor."

"Please. Oh, God, help them." Nina covered her face as two shots rang out. Sharp pieces of brick sliced through her skirt and dug into her knees. Thuds told her the bodies had fallen into the street. The footsteps faded, and she opened her eyes. The soldiers had moved on, leaving behind the broken bodies. What was happening to the city she loved? Had God abandoned them?

"Ma'am?" A strong hand grasped her elbow and pulled her to her feet.

Nina let her hands fall from her eyes and stared into the

face of the soldier who'd covered her body with his during the violent aftershock. "They shot them in cold blood."

"Excuse me?" Cerulean-blue eyes peered from a face coated with dust. "Shot who? Are you hurt?"

She shook off his hand. "Not me, Sergeant. Your men shot two civilians while they stood, in danger, on top of that building." Her words stuck on a sob. "Now they lie among the bricks like unwanted garbage!"

"I'm sorry you had to see that." The sergeant guided her to an abandoned chair and helped her sit. "Here, drink this." He handed her a canteen.

Nina twisted off the cap and turned up the canteen. She rinsed her mouth and spat in the dirt, mortified that such an action was necessary. Then she gulped the cool water. It eased the dryness of her throat. "Thank you. For the water and for your protection earlier."

"So, it is you." He squatted in front of her. "I wondered. I'm Sergeant Jacob Taft. I thought I should introduce myself since we seem to keep running into each other."

"Nina Hansen."

"Where are the children?"

She sighed. "On the ferry and away from this place of death and destruction."

"Why did you stay, ma'am, if you don't mind my asking?"

"I want to help, and I want to photograph what's happening." Her shoulders slumped. "There's more happening than I bargained for." The memory of the bodies hitting the ground sent a shiver through her. "And I'm looking for a place to volunteer."

"You aren't looking in the right place." He stood and held out a hand. "What do you want to help with?"

"Wherever I'm needed the most."

Chapter 3

Jacob's heart had stopped when he'd seen the pretty woman kneeling in a pile of rock. Crying women were not his specialty.

"I'm headed to the Golden Gate Park," he said. "Several thousand refugees are already there. I'm sure your help in handing out food and water will be greatly appreciated. Plus, you'll be given shelter until you can find permanent accommodations."

"Thank you." Her tears stopped and a sad smile graced her face. Despite the dirt on her cheeks and forehead, she was the most beautiful woman he'd ever seen. "I'll walk with you."

Jacob's mouth dried up. If not for the mountain of responsibility on his shoulders, he might have considered enjoying her company. He had planned on having someone else walk her to camp. "I didn't mean to say that I'm headed there immediately." He glanced around for a soldier who would relish the opportunity to escort a pretty girl. He stiffened, remembering what she'd said. "What do you mean my men shot two civilians?"

He clenched his jaw as she recounted her story. "Were they drinking?" Orders or not, as the day's horrors escalated, even his soldiers would turn to the mind-numbing effects of alcohol.

"I didn't think to check." Her eyes widened. "Do you think they were? How can they protect us if they're drunk?"

"Let's go." Jacob took her by the elbow and herded her down the street. They needed to move. The camp was still a distance away, and the fire was getting closer and building in intensity. Any avenue of escape could be cut off in a moment. "I'm sure the soldiers had no choice. Would you rather be shot or burn to death?"

"Neither." Her voice squeaked.

He didn't want to go to the refugee camp yet. The city needed him patrolling the streets, especially if what Miss Hansen said was true. As time passed, and tensions grew, men were prone to shoot first and ask questions later. Maybe he could prevent some innocent deaths if he were present.

Lost in his thoughts, several minutes passed before he realized Miss Hansen had chattered nonstop since they had started walking. "Pardon me?"

"How does the city intend to stop the fire?" She paused to snap a photo of a cat, kitten in its mouth, climbing a mountain of debris. "It's noon, and whole blocks are flaming. The fire will continue until it has nothing left to feed on."

Did she think him stupid? "Of course it will. With burst gas pipes and broken water mains, the fire department has its hands full. Thankfully, San Francisco has one of the best fire departments in the nation. My job is to supervise the camp once night falls."

"It isn't night." She glanced up at him. "Please don't think we need to hurry on my account. I'm content to take pictures while you work."

She wanted to follow him around the dangerous streets? Not a wise decision, even for a woman displaying the bravery this one did. Finding someone to escort her became a top priority, especially as a black cloud of smoke lingered over the city. His eyes watered.

"Follow me, Miss Hansen."

"God bless you, Sergeant."

Jacob scowled. "If God were blessing us, ma'am, San Francisco wouldn't be lying in ruin right now."

"If God weren't blessing you, Sergeant, you could be dead." She lifted her chin.

Two men patrolled the next block. Jacob waved his arm, determined to get the defiant woman to safety, regardless of her desire to take photos. "Private!"

"Yes, sir!" The man jogged closer and saluted.

"Please escort this woman to Golden Gate Park. Put her in touch with someone in charge. She's willing to help." Jacob nodded at Nina. "Ma'am. I'm sure we'll see each other again."

He turned back to the soldier. "Straight to the camp, Private. No loitering."

"But, sir—" the woman protested.

"No arguments. Off with you, now." He watched them turn the corner and expelled a deep breath. He shouldn't be short with the woman. She had only wanted to help. But allowing her to follow him about the dangerous city would be foolish on his part.

A shot rang out. He whirled, trying to gauge its location. A scream pierced the air from the block east of him. Jacob rushed in that direction.

He found Miss Hansen cowered under the awning of a drugstore, while the private faced down two armed men. The fire was only two doors down. They didn't have time for this nonsense.

He fired a shot in the air. "Clear out or be shot!"

"We ain't got no intentions of leaving." One of the men,

a burly man in a bathrobe and trousers, transferred his attention to Jacob. "My wife needs medicine that's in that store. I aim to get it for her." His gaze flicked down the street. "And I'd like to get it before we all burn."

"We have orders, Sergeant." The private shook his rifle. "Orders to shoot looters."

Jacob chewed the inside of his cheek. He had no desire to shoot the two men. Instead, he sympathized with the man's need to retrieve medicine for his wife. Making a snap decision, he motioned his head. "Go on, but get only what you need."

"Sir?" The private frowned.

"I take full responsibility. Continue on with Miss Hansen." He groaned as he realized that during the time it had taken for him to decide how to proceed, she'd taken pictures. Wonderful. A photo of two armed soldiers facing down two armed civilians. That would be on the front page of every newspaper in the country.

Crackling flames filled the air. "Private, make haste." Jacob watched him lead Miss Hansen away before stepping into the dim recesses of the store. "Mister, it's time to go."

"Thank you, sir." The bathrobed man joined his friend on the street, clutching a paper sack. "God bless you."

Jacob strongly suspected the bag also contained medicine of a different nature. Perhaps to numb the effects of the nightmare around them. Drunk or not, the men didn't deserve to be shot.

He quickened his pace and turned east, hoping to outrun the licking flames. He couldn't go to the camp yet. Not until he was sure there were no civilians stuck in the fire's path.

Fire was always the enemy. Maybe it had beaten his parents and younger sister, but Jacob wouldn't back down now. Now he found himself thrust into the place of his darkest nightmares. He wasn't responsible for one person, but for thousands. He clenched his trembling hands into fists.

More gunfire rattled a street away. Jacob sprinted toward the sound.

"Wait." Nina held out her arm to stop the private with her. "I want to go to Nob Hill."

He shook his head. "Ma'am, I have my orders."

"Just for a moment." If she stood up there, she could see the whole city and get a powerful panorama shot. "Then I'll let you take me to the camp. I promise. Please, I have to record today's events." How else could she process the horror around her? Taking pictures, developing them, maybe sending them to newspapers across the country. She needed to do something to inform others about the catastrophe. She needed to help in some small way.

She wasn't a nurse. There was little she could do until people actually filed into camp. From the crowd in the streets, it didn't look to her like many of them had left the city yet, fire or not.

"My orders are to bring you to camp." He reached out to take her by the arm.

She dodged his grasp. "Will you shoot me if I don't obey? Please, I promise it's only for a short time."

He glanced about them, then nodded and set off at a brisk pace.

By the time they reached the hill, Nina's stomach rumbled with hunger. She surveyed the clusters of people picnicking, and her shoulders slumped. How could they act as if they were on a Sunday outing? Hadn't they seen the destruction below? The people and animals crushed by falling brick and stone? Tears burned her eyes at their apathy.

"What is your name, Private?" She swallowed past the lump in her throat.

"John Moore, ma'am."

"Well, Private Moore. What do you make of this scene?" Nina snapped a picture. "It's rather heartbreaking, isn't it? How people go about their business as if it's nothing more than a summer party."

"Most likely they're in shock, ma'am." He stared rigidly in the direction she pointed. "Folks act strange when they lose everything. Those who still have their possessions often act even stranger. They're unsure how to respond and tend to look on things as entertainment."

"Did you lose anything?"

"I don't know the whereabouts of my parents, ma'am." His Adam's apple bobbed as he swallowed hard.

"I'm sorry." Nina turned and photographed the city skyline, a black cloud hanging over the buildings. "It's sad." She sighed. *Please keep his family safe, Lord.* "I'm ready to go to the camp now." She couldn't take another minute of the scene in front of her.

Could she even hear God's voice over the clamor of fire engines and the roar of the inferno? She looked at her camera. Taking photographs seemed so frivolous. Would the pictures matter in the long run? Not as much as the people in them, perhaps, but recording the events for history had to be worth something.

Without speaking, she followed the private until they reached the park. Already, hundreds of white tents flapped in the afternoon breeze. "Thank you for bringing me."

Private Moore nodded. "My pleasure." He backed up a step, turned away and marched back toward the fire.

Nina watched him leave, lifting up a prayer for his safety and the others fighting the fire, then hitched her skirts and strode toward a middle-aged woman standing behind a table. Brown boxes of food were piled behind her. Over her head hung a sign that read, Commit No Nuisance. No Smoking in or about Tents. No LIQUORS Will Be Allowed in Camp.

"I'm here to help," Nina said. "Whatever you need me to do, I'll do."

"God bless you. I'm Mabel Stoltz." The woman gave her a weary smile. "Come behind the table with me. Every family that comes through, we give them a tent. If they are single, we have women's and men's tents set up at the back of the camp. Also, everyone, even children, get water and a box of food."

"I'm Nina Hansen."

"Are you alone?"

Nina nodded and squeezed past a pile of folded tents. "I am now. Until this morning, I worked at the Maria Kip Orphanage. They left the city, and I stayed behind."

"Those poor dears." Mrs. Stoltz handed a tent to a man with a bandage on his head, and then directed him to a Red Cross tent opposite their table. "The larger wood building is a temporary hospital. We're glad to have you."

By nightfall, Nina's limbs trembled with fatigue and a headache pounded the backs of her eyes. She plucked her soiled blouse away from her skin. She'd give anything for a bath. Maybe she could find enough water to at least wash her face. Plopping into a chair, she leaned back and closed her eyes. The stream of refugees continued, while she and Mrs. Stoltz took turns seeing to their needs.

"Miss Hansen?"

Nina opened her eyes. "Johnny!" She leaped to her feet and grabbed him to her. "What happened? Why are you still here?"

"My brother dashed off before we boarded." Tears welled in his eyes. "I left to look for him. By the time we returned, the ferry had gone and no more are coming. The docks are too damaged and the ferries are needed for the military they keep bringing in."

His younger brother, Sam, peeked around him. "I'm sorry. I saw a puppy." He held out a mixed-breed pup barely old enough to be without its mother. Ah, there was the mom, watching from between Johnny's legs.

Nina knelt in front of Sam. "Oh, dear." She wrapped the six-year-old in a hug. "Let's get you two fed. You can stay with me."

Mrs. Stoltz handed her a tent. "Guess you got a family to care for now, bless you."

"Guess I do." Her heart swelled. She handed her new home to Johnny. "Find a place to pitch this and tie this ribbon somewhere close by so I can find you." She tugged the blue scrap of dirty silk from what was left of her bun. Having the boys to call family, even if temporarily, meant the world to her, but having the responsibility of two children during a major disaster also left her chilled.

The line of people flocking to the park seemed to never end. Nina's heart ached for every misplaced family. Some of them posted notices on the trees, asking for news of a loved one.

She scanned the field of tents. Living in close quarters was sure to breed disease, and only the good Lord knew what kind of diabolical behaviors men would exhibit.

"Go get some rest." Mrs. Stoltz placed her hands on her hips and leaned back. "Relief is coming."

Two women hurried forward, faces washed and hands clean. Nina perked up. "Is there water to wash?"

One of them nodded. "A rain barrel of seawater is by the workers' tent. You can't clean your clothes, but at least you can get rid of some of the soot from your face."

Nina sped in that direction. How wonderful would a clean face feel? She passed a sign stating in nine differ-

ent languages: Do Not Spit. Another hung over a barrel:
You May Spit Here.

Why the warnings? Her skin crawled at what the messages could mean. A rat scuttled past. She shrieked and
jumped aside. How many creatures would flock to the
camp in an effort to outrun the fire?

When she finally located the rain barrel for washing,
she almost skipped. She closed her eyes and poured the
cool water over her face, letting it run down her blouse.
She'd worry about clean clothes tomorrow. With water
dripping down her face, she placed her hands on each side
of the barrel and hung her head. Tears mingled with the
sea as she cried.

Images of the people and animals she'd seen bombarded
her mind. She swallowed back bile. So many injured or
dead. Maybe she should've gone with Mrs. Fox. But then,
she wouldn't have been here for Johnny and Sam. Clearly,
God had a purpose in her decision to stay. She straightened and took a deep breath.

Thankfully, the breeze blew away from the camp, giving a respite to the smoky air. She increased her pace and
sighed when she spotted the flimsy strip of blue flapping
from a tent. A person wouldn't be able to snore without
keeping their neighbor awake, but at least there'd be something between them and the elements. She parted the flap
and gaped. Three mattresses and blankets lay side by side
on the ground.

Johnny grinned. "I found some other boys to help me
fetch the ones we tossed out of the orphanage building.
Got you a change of clothes, too, Miss Hansen. I don't
know if they're yours or not, but I know how much you
hate being dirty."

Nina planted a big kiss on his dirty cheek. "You are my
hero, Johnny Smith. A true hero."

He beamed. "I figured I might as well take what I could before the fire got it." He lay back and folded his arms behind his head. "The fire department is having a heck of a time. They've taken to using water from the holes in the road. They're also carting it from the sea. But it's too late. I saw dynamite in the back of a wagon. That might be interesting to see."

Dynamite! Nina fell to the mattress beside a sleeping Sam. What would they think of next? She rubbed a hand over the rough fabric of her bed. Would Johnny's actions be considered looting?

She'd fight for the material comforts. Who knew when things would get better? Entire city blocks would fall victim to the fire's tenacity. It would take months, years, to rebuild. She threw an arm over her eyes, too tired to shed more tears.

How were the soldiers doing? Sergeant Taft and Sergeant Moore? Had the latter found his family?

"You okay, Miss Hansen?"

She opened her eyes to see Johnny and Sam, bending over her, their faces creased with concern. "Yes, I'm just exhausted."

"I bet you've seen some horrors today, too." Johnny lay down on his own mattress. "I know I did. There were these draft horses, lying in the street, crushed by the weight of blocks from a nearby building." His voice trembled. "The people are bad enough, but the poor animals are lost. That's why I let Sam take the pup. Tomorrow, I'm hunting rats with the mama dog. There's bound to be lots of rats in camp the more people we get."

Nina's eyes widened. Rats! Heaven help them. She'd get no sleep that night.

Chapter 4

Nina stood outside her tent the next morning and glanced around the milling crowd for Johnny and Sam. No doubt they were already hunting rats. She shuddered. Somehow, she needed to find a way to feed her charges, while seeing where she could help the homeless, and still find time to take her photographs.

A few feet away, Sergeant Taft argued with a man who was bleeding profusely from his head. The sergeant was trying to convince the poor gentleman that he was in no condition to venture into the city to fight fires. When Taft handed him a dirty bandage, Nina wondered whether it would do more harm than good. The man hastily wrapped the cloth around his head.

"If you don't go to the medical tent," Sergeant Taft said, "I'll have you escorted." Noticing Nina, the sergeant waved her over. "Please make sure this man gets medical attention."

Nina nodded and linked her arm through the wounded man's. "You'll make a wonderful model for a photograph. A brave man like you, injured while helping others. Why, you'll be famous!" Her face heated under Sergeant Taft's approving smile. The man was quite handsome when he wasn't scowling. She watched him march away, his strides long and purposeful, before turning to the man in her care.

What would it be like to know Sergeant Taft outside of such a disastrous occurrence?

"You think so, miss?" The man's eyes widened. "Do you reckon I'll get my picture in the newspapers back east?"

"I don't see why not." Nina deposited him at the medical tent. As a nurse unwound the filthy makeshift bandage, Nina took the beaming man's picture. After saying goodbye, she headed out of the camp and into the chaotic city.

She'd give herself one hour for pictures, then report for duty at the camp. While her photographs were important to her, serving the lost and injured must take priority.

A massive explosion erupted a few streets over from the Mission District where Nina made her way around toppled buildings. She covered her ears and crouched in a doorway. The entire city would be blown apart if the explosions continued.

Several minutes later, she passed a convent where a group of elderly nuns rushed to load crosses, statues and other sacred items into a wagon. Nina snapped a picture and, since several men helped the nuns remove items from the building, she continued on her way, keeping a close eye on the time so as not to be late for her shift with the Red Cross.

A wagon filled with household goods blocked the road. A man and woman tried removing a wooden chest. The driver swiped at them with a riding crop. "Nothing is removed until you pay me the twenty-five dollars."

"That's highway robbery," the other man said. "Other draymen are charging only five."

"Please, sir," the woman pleaded. "All that we own is in your wagon. Please let us unload and hire someone else. We cannot afford your charges."

Nina stepped forward. "Are you trying to swindle these poor people while fires rage out of control? Shame on you."

"Stay out of it, miss." The drayman clicked the reins to his team of horses.

"Absolutely not." Nina grabbed the bridle of the horse nearest to her. "You'll have to drag me."

"That won't stop me." He raised his whip.

"Maybe this will." Sergeant Taft stepped around the wagon, a pistol aimed at the driver. "If the folks want to remove their belongings, they have every right to, and five dollars to drive these good people to their destination is better than none in your pocket, don't you think?"

The driver sighed. "Five dollars it is."

The man and woman climbed onto the seat next to the driver and waved as the wagon pulled away. Nina smiled and turned to thank the sergeant. "It seems you are always coming to my rescue."

"Are you crazy?" He asked, gripping her by the elbow and leading her out of the street. "Grabbing the bridle? That man could have run over you."

"I only intended to keep him from driving away." She yanked free. "Thank you for your assistance, Sergeant." She whirled and marched away.

He jogged to her side. "I'm sorry, Miss Hansen, but you mustn't put yourself needlessly in harm's way."

She stopped suddenly enough for him to run into her. She faced him. "You believe keeping someone from being robbed is needless? What is your purpose in the city, Sergeant?"

"To keep order and run the refugee camp as efficiently as possible." He squared his shoulders. "I'm also to keep the foolish from doing anything foolhardy."

"Foolish!" Had he just called her a fool? "Good day, sir!" With a swish of her skirts, she resumed her march down the street.

"Please accept my apologies," he said, once again catching up with her. "We could work well together, I think. Especially back at the camp."

"Are you expecting me to stay in camp?" Despite his handsomeness, she was no longer sure she wanted to spend more time with him. Not with his surly, bossy manner.

"Yes, ma'am."

"Then you will be disappointed." She stopped to snap a photo of a building leaning so far to the side that the top eave rested upon the ground. "I have more than one duty during this catastrophe, and short of arresting me, you won't be able to change my mind."

"That is unfortunate." The sergeant removed his hat and ran his fingers through his hair. "I witnessed you caring for the orphans and heard, just this morning, about a group of Chinese refugees from a Mission house. I had hoped you could help with the poor girls."

Oh, the man was good. He knew how to wrench Nina's heart. "Girls?"

"Rescued from lives of prostitution."

The sparkle in his eyes told Nina he believed he had her right where he wanted her. "I would be more than happy to help them. I have two boys from the orphanage staying with me now, but I'll do what I can. Right after I finish taking my daily photographs."

Another blast of dynamite sent her stumbling into his arms and into a chest as solid as the wall next to her. Would dynamite really stop the fires by leveling buildings? Her neck flushed and she stepped back. "Pardon me. The explosions tend to frighten me."

"No apology necessary. Holding you in my arms is becoming a pleasant regularity." He replaced his hat and smiled. "Since we'll be working together, please call me Jacob."

"I'm Nina." What a rogue! Teasing her as if she'd thrown

herself at him. She lifted her chin. "I'm afraid my morning has resulted in very few photographs. I must report to the Red Cross tent now."

"I will escort you."

She raised a hand in protest. "I know the way."

"I insist. It isn't safe for a woman to be out alone, day or night."

While normally she'd like the attentions of a handsome man, Nina had more important things to do than be treated as a helpless female. "I'll be fine." With a determined step in her walk, she headed for camp, leaving Jacob on the uneven sidewalk. Hopefully, she'd let him know she wouldn't be bossed around.

Her stomach rumbled, reminding her she hadn't had breakfast. She mentally made a list of things she wanted to accomplish that day, first of all seeing whether she could find out where Johnny and Sam had gotten off to. She wasn't worried about them not eating. The older brother would know to seek aid for Sam, if not for himself. She could get food at the Red Cross tent. After her shift, she would search for the Chinese refugees and see how she could lessen their burden. She was reminded again of why she hadn't left on the ferry with Mrs. Fox. There were so many here that she could help.

Her day filled with purpose, she entered the camp with a smile on her face.

"You're awfully chipper this morning," Mabel Stoltz said, returning her smile. "I've saved a biscuit and a bit of dry cheese for you after seeing you duck out of camp earlier."

"God bless you." Nina devoured the meager breakfast with thanksgiving in her heart. She eyed the seemingly never ending line of refugees. "How many people do you think are here?"

"I heard upwards of two hundred thousand." She handed an elderly woman a threadbare blanket. "We don't have enough supplies."

"I'll ask the sergeant in charge what we can do about that the next time I see him." Nina handed a tin of canned meat to the next person in line. So many people, so little food. And water would quickly become a major concern.

As the afternoon sped by and supplies dwindled, Nina kept an eye out for Jacob. Several times throughout the day, she spotted Johnny and Sam running through the camp, the pup scampering after them. Johnny had a burlap bag swung over his shoulder. Nina had no desire to ask what he carried, for fear it was full of rodents.

Nina blinked as a group of young girls, heads down and shepherded like sheep by a burly man, passed by. Could they be some of the girls she had promised to help? They didn't look much older than Johnny, and a couple of them a year or so younger.

Mabel snorted. "Women of ill repute."

"Really?" Nina craned her neck to see them better. "Surely not. They're only children."

"You, my dear, are naive. You wait and see. Life in this camp just took a turn for the worse."

Everything in Jacob had wanted to follow Nina and make sure she made it safely to camp, but duty called. His orders were to patrol the city for part of the day and manage the camp for the rest. He had soldiers under his command, and a lot of them would take too many breaks if he didn't monitor them. With a heavy sigh, he followed the sound of the dynamite blasts to Harris Street. He approached the young man with the badge, and watched as he ordered a fine Victorian home to be blasted. "In a few minutes," the young man said, "all of these houses will be up in the air."

"Why?" Jacob asked. "None of these homes are in danger."

"My orders are to dynamite this block, so dynamite it, we will."

"Surely, the goal is to save as many structures as possible? Men strived for hours to save these homes. Can't you honor their sacrifice?"

"But, the mayor…"

"I will speak to the mayor myself." Jacob clapped the young man on the shoulder.

"Please, son," a well-dressed man said. "I'm Dr. Bledsoe, and this is my home." He handed over a bottle of wine. "For seeing reason."

The young man took the bottle and rushed down the street.

Jacob shook hands with the doctor. Another catastrophe averted. Although, now he needed to speak to the mayor. He'd rather deal with the stubborn Miss Hansen than the city government's fools.

He stopped at the corner of a partially gutted brick building and read the paper tacked there.

PROCLAMATION BY THE MAYOR

The Federal Troops, the members of the Regular Police Force and all Special Police Officers have been authorized by me to KILL any and all persons found engaged in Looting or in the Commission of Any Other Crime.

I have directed all the Gas and Electric Lighting Co.'s not to turn on Gas or Electricity until I order them to do so. You may therefore expect the city to remain in darkness for an indefinite time.

I request all citizens to remain at home from darkness until daylight every night until order is restored.

I WARN all Citizens of the danger of fire from Damaged or Destroyed Chimneys, Broken or Leaking Gas Pipes or Fixtures, or any like cause.

E. E. SCHMITZ, MAYOR

Dated, April 18, 1906

Martial law had been declared. Jacob turned toward camp, his heart heavy. He hadn't gone two blocks before hearing tales of instant executions. Jacob increased his steps, hoping that Nina had heeded his orders to return to camp. He wouldn't put it past some trigger-happy fellow to shoot first and ask questions later, whether the victim be male or female. To lose such a fine, brave, young woman would be disastrous indeed. The city needed more people like her.

By the time he reached the outskirts of town, dusk had settled and fires occupied half the city. Despite setting off dynamite in an attempt to stop the fire's progress, it continued to blaze through buildings. Occasional gunshots rang over the mayhem.

His spirits lifted when he spotted Nina hard at work handing out provisions. He looked forward to working with her in their common goal to help the refugees. Maybe, once things returned to normal, *if* they returned to normal, he could pursue a courtship. He'd be out of the service by then and ready to settle down. If, and it was a mighty big if, he could leave behind his fears of commitment and responsibility.

"Jacob!" Nina motioned him to the tent, her lovely face creased with worry.

"Is something wrong?"

"We're quickly running out of provisions." She laid a

hand on his arm. His skin tingled from her touch. "Please tell me you know of a place we can get more."

"I do, maybe." He stepped away from her. He didn't need or want the emotions that arose from her touch. The Presidio housed a basement full of supplies. If no one had confiscated them yet, it was very likely he could ask for the crates of provisions. "Are you willing to accompany me in the morning?"

Pink dusted her cheeks. "I'd feel privileged. Anything to help these poor souls."

He would have liked her to feel pleasure at spending time in his company, but would take what he could get. Jacob shook his head. He was an addle-brained fool. One moment he wanted to see more of her, the next he wanted to run as far from her presence as possible. Romance had no place in the midst of disaster. He would do well to remember that. "I'll be by your tent at 8 a.m."

A boy approximately fifteen years of age, accompanied by a much younger boy, dashed up to Nina and plopped a full sack at her feet. A strange squeaking emitted from inside the bag. Nipping around the boys' heels were a puppy and the ugliest wire-haired mutt Jacob had ever seen.

"I found my rat-catching dog, Miss Hansen," the older boy said, "and she's a wonder! Look at all the rats we caught. People are paying me a penny for each one I remove from their tent. I bet this pup will grow up to be as good as his mother at catching the rodents."

"Johnny!" Nina planted fists on her hips. "You shouldn't charge for doing a good service."

"They're offering, I promise."

"What do you plan on doing with them…now?" Jacob took a step back. How long would it take one of the rats to chew through the bag? The dog wonder obviously hadn't killed all of them.

"I'm going to drown them in the sea." He sprinted away, the younger boy and dogs following, before Jacob could tell him of the curfew.

Nina sighed. "They're all that's left in San Francisco from the orphanage. They're staying in my tent. I fear Johnny will be my undoing. But he means well."

"You can't begrudge the boy a chance to make a few coins." Jacob admired any young man willing to put in a hard day's work.

"No, but I can hope to instill a charitable heart in him." Nina said goodbye to the older woman at her side and stepped from behind the table. "Many good people are doing deeds for nothing more than a smile."

"Not everyone is as kind as you." He crooked his arm. "May I escort you to your tent?"

"Only if you'll allow me to fix you something to eat. Oh!" She dashed back to the table, grabbed a small box of supplies and rejoined him.

"I can't eat your rations." There was so little to go around as it was.

"Pay back the favor when you can." She smiled, sending his heart racing, and, despite the long day, fairly skipped at his side. Rarely had he seen anything more beautiful than this woman with her stained blouse, smudged cheek and loose hair.

"Oh, look, Jacob, a stove." Nina rushed toward a group of women gathered around a wood-burning stove. "This is much easier than cooking over a simple fire."

And safer. He would try to find her a stove of her own come morning. While she took her turn cooking, he strolled the lanes between the lines of flapping canvas. Already soot, carried on the breeze, marred the once white fabric. If the wind didn't change direction soon, the camp residents would need to wear clothes around their faces and their temporary homes would be in danger of fire. If that happened…how would he get them all safely evacuated?

The realization of how ill-equipped he was to be responsible for so many lives choked him worse than the smoke. He passed a tent where five children under the age of ten played in the dirt. Maybe he couldn't personally help everyone, but he could do some good, starting with one family at a time.

A toddler teetered close to the fire, and Jacob scooped the little boy into his arms. "That's not a good idea, little fella." He handed the child to his frazzled mother. "Is there something you need, ma'am? Perhaps I can get it for you."

"Water to keep the young'uns clean would be a blessing. I don't want to waste the drinking water, but perhaps a pail from the bay?"

He nodded. "I'll send a soldier over first thing in the morning." In fact, he would organize some men to build troughs set up for the purpose of bathing and laundry. Salt water wasn't good for much, but it would at least help to keep the grime out of things. The barrels set up for that purpose were few and far between.

As he made his way back to the wood-burning stove, he found Nina squatting in the dirt, offering a cup of water to a Chinese girl in tattered clothing. The girl darted away, disappearing in the sea of tents.

Sighing, Nina stood. "I fear there may be an illegal prostitution ring set up in your camp, Jacob."

Chapter 5

Nina waited for Jacob outside her tent as Johnny and Sam finished off a breakfast of biscuits with a smear of jam. Her attention kept diverting from the task of caring for the two boys to the small crate she'd discovered next to their tent first thing that morning. She'd wanted to open it immediately, especially after reading the accompanying note from Jacob saying for her to enjoy the items he had managed to procure, but two boys demanding food had caused her to wait.

Using an extra iron tent stake, she pried open the lid. Inside was an extra water container, a couple of cans of tinned meat and a packet of crackers. She smiled. It wasn't a lot, but she was grateful for every bite of food she could put in her charges' mouths. *God bless you, Jacob Taft.*

As if her thoughts had brought him to her, she lifted her head and met his sparkling gaze. "Thank you so much," she said.

He held out a hand to help her to her feet. "My privilege. Food and water will only get harder to come by. When someone works as hard as you do, they need to be rewarded for their service."

Her heart sank. His kindness was payment for her services. Not the gesture of friendship she had hoped.

She shoved aside her disappointment. "Let me put this in the tent, and I'll be ready to go." She lifted the box and set it under one of the cots before hanging her camera around her neck. Once outside again, she gave orders to the boys not to venture from the camp, then followed Jacob into the still-burning city.

"The smoke seems to have increased." She held a hand over her mouth and nose.

"With the broken gas lines, and people not willing to follow orders about not cooking in their homes, the city can't get the fire under control. They're carting in water from the bay." He put a hand on her elbow and guided her over a fissure in the street. "The first day, the fire destroyed most of the government buildings, then yesterday spread to the Mission District. Today, the flames are heading toward Russian Hill and Telegraph Hill."

She gasped. "There will be nothing left."

He frowned. "Not much, that's for sure. But…" He smiled. "The Presidio is still standing, for now. Let's hope there are supplies inside."

"I'll pray for that this minute."

His mouth curled. "You do that."

"You don't believe in prayer?" She could hardly conceive such a thought. Was it possible that the first man she could see herself being in a relationship with didn't share her faith?

"Let's just say it hasn't done me a lot of good in the past."

Her heart ached for him. What had happened to cause such a lack of belief?

They entered the Presidio grounds. If they did find supplies, which didn't seem likely considering the number of hastily erected tents, how could they take from these people to help those in their own camp? Who were they to choose the camp more worthy?

For half the day, they searched building after building, until Nina thought her feet would fall off. They entered the last of two buildings. It looked as if it had been vacant for years—if the layer of dust on the floor was any indication.

Jacob sighed. "Let's check the basement. This search is taking longer than I'd thought. I have other duties to tend to, as you most likely do."

Nina was already late for her shift with the Red Cross. Another hour wouldn't hurt too much. If they were successful in finding something, Mabel would likely forgive her.

Their feet kicked up dust as they descended the steep staircase. Sunlight filtering through grime-coated windows provided just enough light for them to see crates piled against the walls. Her heart skipped a beat. Had they finally found something useful?

Jacob rushed to the crates and opened one. Inside was a wonderful pile of army surplus blankets. "Jackpot!" He stepped back and glanced again at the crates. "There must be two thousand blankets here."

Nina clapped. "We should share them with this camp, don't you think? After all, we found them here."

"Great idea. This will provide comfort to a lot of refugees. I'll run out and find someone in authority. Will you be all right here alone?"

She nodded. "I'll look around a bit more." She wasn't afraid of the dark or enclosed spaces. Mrs. Fox had taught all the orphans from as far back as Nina could remember not to fear what the earthly world could throw at them, not if God was on their side.

While she waited, she dug behind empty barrels and toppled boxes, discovering a case of military rations. It wasn't a lot, but every bit helped. Maybe Jacob would consider keeping this for his men. After all, they needed the sustenance after working all day in deplorable conditions. By the time she discovered another crate of rations, Jacob had returned with three soldiers.

"We have permission to take half of these," he said.

She told him about the rations, and he agreed the enlisted men needed them more than anyone. "You did great, Nina." He patted her shoulder, sending a rush of heat through her.

She shook away the feeling. The aftermath of an earthquake was not the time for romantic notions. She ducked her head, wanting to hide a face she knew was as red as the sunset, and climbed the stairs into the light. As the men carted the crates up the stairs, she snapped their picture.

"Doesn't that camera get heavy?" Jacob set a crate at her feet.

"Not really. If you have one of these men explain to Mrs. Stoltz that I'm helping you find supplies, I won't have to return right away and can continue to help you." She'd taken so few photographs the past few days and yet, she desperately needed to find a place to develop the ones she had taken. As a last resort, she could mail the negatives directly to a newspaper back east. She was willing to sacrifice keeping some of the copies for herself in order to tell the plight of the people of San Francisco. If she needed to mail the negatives, thus leaving nothing for herself, she would.

Jacob shook his head. "I would prefer you head back to the camp with these soldiers. The streets are dangerous."

"But I'll be with you." She couldn't be safer.

"You'll slow me down."

"I promise I won't."

"What if I get into an altercation?"

"Then I'll step aside like a good girl."

"Ha."

She frowned at his obvious reluctance to trust her. She

needed to convince him. She wasn't ready to return to the camp and, besides, what if there were more children or hurting women that needed her help? They would respond better to a female.

"I can help you, Jacob." She placed a hand on his arm. "Let me try. Please."

He glanced at her hand, then back to her face. A girl could drown in his eyes. Her mouth dried up as they locked gazes for a few seconds. It was like they were the only two people in the city.

He sighed, breaking the spell. "Just this once, but if you hinder me, or get into danger, this will be the last time you accompany me."

"Deal." She thrust out her hand, trying not to show pleasure at how it felt in his larger one. She would make sure he didn't regret his decision.

They left the Presidio and headed in a direction different from the way they had come, into utter devastation. What the earthquake hadn't destroyed, the fires did. Once beautiful homes lay in ruins, either by flame or dynamite.

Nina sniffed back tears. Her beloved city resembled a shadow of itself. She stepped closer to Jacob, taking reassurance from his strong presence. Each explosion caused her to jump. She clutched her camera like a lifeline, doing her best to record this historical event.

People wandered the streets, dazed and lost. Jacob tried to steer them to the refugee camps, but many of them shook their heads and continued to rummage through what was once their home.

Nina searched for something happy to photograph, other than the hopelessness so many people portrayed. Where was the strength and fortitude associated with the American people?

A massive smoke cloud rose over the buildings. A crowd

of people froze and watched as the cloud drifted closer. Nina stepped away from Jacob in order to snap the scene. Seconds later, he yanked her out of the way of a fire carriage thundering toward the blaze. She tripped the camera's shutter again.

She took a photo of Jacob, outlined by towering flames. Oh, how she wished she could capture the picture in color. She whirled at the joyful cry of a child and snapped a photo of a young girl pulling a rag doll from beneath a pile of debris. The child hugged the toy as if it was a long lost family member. The little girl's smile brightened even the smoke-filled street. Nina finally had a picture of hope.

"Oakland and Berkeley felt the shake, too," a private stated, standing at attention in front of Jacob. "But damage appears to be minimal."

"That's the first good news I've heard all day." Jacob pulled a handkerchief from his pocket and wiped his brow. The once pristine fabric showed stains and streaks of soot. Cleanliness was going to be difficult under the current circumstances. "Are you able to send civilians to one of the camps?"

"We're doing our best, sir, but some refuse to leave."

"I've experienced that myself, unfortunately. Change the request to a mandatory order. Unless their home is untouched, they must leave it behind." Safety came first, despite some people's silly ideas of salvaging personal property.

An elderly Chinese woman herded four young girls down the street. The crimson and gold of the woman's dress showed in stark contrast to the burned buildings. Jacob frowned as the women headed for the Presidio. Could Nina be correct in her assumption of a prostitution ring? He'd chosen to ignore her statement the evening before, not believing anyone could be so bold as to open a prostitution ring in his camp, but now he wondered whether he'd been remiss in dismissing her idea so quickly.

The Chinese girls shot frightened sideways glances in his direction, strengthening his opinion they weren't out for an innocent stroll. But what could he do about it without any proof?

Nina lifted her camera to take their photograph and Jacob put a hand over the lens. "No. The lead woman will be angry if you take their picture."

"Why?"

"They are supposed to remain hidden. For them to walk the streets at this time of the day means their destination is very important."

"I want to help them. I will help them, somehow." The determined look on Nina's face chilled his heart. If she got involved with the dirty underbelly of Chinatown— How could he protect her if she insisted on going where he told her not to? He shook his head. The stubborn woman meant more to him than she should. They'd known each other for only three days, yet it seemed much longer.

Was she his opportunity to redeem himself? If he were to keep Nina safe, could he finally leave behind his feelings of inadequacy and failure?

"Leave them be." He turned back to the private, gave him a few more orders, and marched for the Golden Gate camp where he intended to deposit Nina into the capable hands of Mrs. Stoltz.

"Are we finished touring the city?" Nina's skirts swished around her ankles.

"You are." Jacob helped her over a pile of fallen bricks.

"Whatever for? I've conformed to your expectations." She pulled free.

"You were almost run down by a fire engine. You almost insulted a Chinese woman. And you've been on the verge of tears more than once." Why couldn't she understand the city streets were not safe for a woman at present? It was all Jacob could do to watch over the handful of men under his leadership and a refugee camp busting at the seams. The last thing he needed was the responsibility of a hopeful beauty determined to help everyone she came into contact with.

She glared and marched ahead, entering the camp. She whirled to face him. "You can go now. I'll be perfectly safe."

He doubted that very seriously, but at least she was out of the fire danger and the possibility of having a building fall on her head. He nodded and left her be. A massive dark cloud blocked the sun, matching his mood. Despite the danger she caused by following him around, Nina brightened his day.

Since he was back in camp, he might as well walk the perimeter and try to get Nina's injured expression out of his mind. It was better that she be angry with him and safe, than pleased and injured…or dead.

"No cooking this close to the tents." He marched to where a disheveled woman cooked over an open fire too near her small tent. They had enough fires to worry about. If one broke out in the camp, they would be doomed. "Cook in the walkway or in the common area, preferably the common area."

"I don't want anyone taking what's mine." She glared. "We've little enough as it is."

Jacob kicked dirt over the fire, not wishing to waste her precious store of water. "Then leave one of your children to guard the tent while you cook. This is nonnegotiable."

The woman started to say something else, then thinking better of it, picked up her pot of watery stew. She rebuilt a fire in the center of the area between the rows of tents.

So be it. At least it was better than inside her canvas home.

"Sir!" A private dashed to Jacob's side and handed him a handwritten note.

After sending the young man away, Jacob unfolded the paper. With two hundred and fifty thousand refugees, his orders were to now oversee the camp and leave the soldiers to someone else. He groaned and slipped the paper into his pocket. His worst nightmare had come true. Instead of helping the city rebuild, it was now up to him, solely, with occasional help from the Presidio, to make sure everyone in the camp was safe and able to survive.

He continued his march down the rows of tents. So many people, and one of them a girl he cared too much about.

He hadn't been able to save his family from a house fire. How could anyone expect him to care for this many people while fires raged mere blocks from their temporary homes?

The memory of his mother's and sister's screams reverberated in his head. The scars on Jacob's back burned. He'd begged his father to let him help, but he had ordered the young Jacob to stay outside while he had run into the house in an attempt to save the others. His father had never emerged from the flames again, leaving Jacob orphaned and alone at the age of fifteen.

He had been the same age as Nina's young friend. If Jacob failed to keep her safe, not only would his heart shatter at the loss of such a wonderful woman, but he would leave two boys alone in a wounded city. He couldn't let that happen.

He stopped by a water barrel and splashed his face vigorously in an attempt to erase the memories. From a tent down the line, someone sang a hymn. Jacob shook his head. God could have saved his family and had chosen not to. That wasn't something Jacob could shrug off.

"Jacob!" Nina strolled toward him, the late afternoon sun highlighting her hair with gold.

Glad for the diversion, he forced a smile to his face. "Is your shift over?"

"I hardly had time to do much. The camp is full now, and my services handing out preliminary supplies are no longer needed, since supplies are running out and a few stores have reopened." She held up her camera. "I've decided to follow you around each day and photograph life in the camp."

He stared. She couldn't be serious. As time progressed, life in the camps could possibly take a nasty turn. Sickness could spread, fights could break out. She should focus on caring for the two boys who lived with her. "I think you're needed elsewhere."

"No." She shook her head, her eyes wide with innocence. "Johnny and Sam are gone all day hunting rats. The rusty can he found is half-full of pennies already. They don't need me other than mealtimes. I'm free to help you."

How could he tell her he didn't want her help? Being in close proximity with her day after day would allow emotions to surface. Emotions he had no desire to experience. There was no room in his heart for romance, no matter his previous attraction. He would admire her bravery and willingness to help others, but no more. He needed to guard his heart to protect her. Everyone he'd ever cared about had died because of him. Despite his earlier resolve to court Nina, such thoughts were nothing more than daydreams until life resumed its normal routine.

"I can help the women relate better to your orders." Was she still talking? "Women and children often respond better to a female, don't you think?"

"You've said that before and the answer is the same. I can't have you in danger."

She frowned. "I'm an adult. I'm capable of making my own decisions. If you're so worried about my safety, don't you think I'd be safer with you than alone?"

He shook his head and turned, continuing down the row of tents. Nina followed, chattering about all the ways she planned to help him. He closed his eyes for a moment and took a deep breath.

"Jacob, I've heard you're now in charge of only the camp. That's a huge responsibility. You'll be glad for my assistance. You'll see." She puffed in her effort to keep up with him. "With the money Johnny is making, we'll be able to afford better living arrangements, once they become available, of course. How long do you think the fires will burn? How long until we are allowed back into the city?"

"Not for years."

"Years! Really?" She halted, then dashed to his side. "Are you poking fun?"

He stopped and faced her. "There is nothing funny about this situation."

"Of course there isn't, but joy can be found in almost any circumstance. Listen, someone is singing."

"I hear them." He continued his fast march.

"Have you heard the laughter of children? Seen a mother tenderly wipe the dirt from her child's face with the hem of her apron?" She put a hand on his arm, turning him to face her.

He stared into her bright eyes, willing himself not to get sucked into what she was saying.

"Life continues, Jacob, and with that life is joy."

"Life brings pain."

"Pain means you're alive."

Chapter 6

As Nina watched yet another mother's children while the woman cooked her family's meal, she wondered whether Jacob had purposely come up with extra chores for her in order to keep her from following him around camp. She hadn't taken near enough photographs, but had managed to send the negatives of the ones she had taken back east on a military mail carrier.

It wasn't that she minded helping those who needed her, not at all, but she wanted to do more. Why couldn't she spend part of her day photographing and the other half serving? After two weeks of virtually no photo taking, she was going a bit crazy.

Not to mention how much she enjoyed spending time with him. It wasn't often Nina met a man as caring and strong as Jacob. Now that she had, she didn't want to let him go. He was just like the heroes in the stories Mrs. Fox read to the children of the orphanage, and he acted as if he couldn't bear her company. She swallowed back the sting of tears. Surely, he didn't enjoy being alone all the time.

Life in the camp had settled into a routine, of sorts. Life did go on, after all, and she wanted to capture every minute of it. She'd have to settle with taking pictures in between the wild-goose chases Jacob sent her on.

Speaking of the man. He strolled by where she sat, a

smile on his face, and nodded to the returning mother. Nina
leaped to her feet, handed the infant to his mother and ran
after Jacob. "What do you have against me helping you?"

He looked surprised. "You are helping me."

"I want to patrol the camp with you."

He frowned. "It's too dangerous. There are fights, gambling and other illegal activities. It's my job to clear out
these unsavory characters. I can't have you in harm's way."

"Stop saying that." He treated her like a child! "That is
my decision to make."

"No, it's mine." He stopped walking. "We're friends,
aren't we?"

"Why…yes, of course." Although lately, she had started
looking at him as much more than a friend.

After two weeks of working side by side, seeing to the
refugees' needs and directing them to the camps when
they encountered them in the city, offering aid in any other
way they could, Nina had seen the kind of man Jacob was.
He might bluster and puff out his chest, but inside beat a
kind heart. One that cared for those under his protection.

"So, I care for you a great deal. I can't in all good con-
scious let you wander the places I must go." He put his
hands on her shoulders. "Please, trust me."

So, he did care for her. As a friend, or as one would look
upon a younger sister. She sighed and nodded. Someday,
he would look at her as a woman; as an equal. If he would
only loosen his rigid opinion on what her role should be,
they could be partners, maybe more than friends.

What would he do if he knew her tent was bursting at
the seams with lost children? So many had been orphaned
after the quake, and with no building large enough to house
them…why, she had no other choice but to care for them.
She wanted to let him know, if for no other reason than

that she needed more supplies. Fortunately, Mrs. Stoltz helped where she could. They'd manage.

Nina would have to follow Jacob's orders and do what she could elsewhere. She'd patrol for people in need on her own. She'd done fine so far. But she would love to have his support.

"Very well." With a hitch of her skirts, she headed home to relieve Johnny so he could hunt for rats. Someone in their "family" needed to make some money.

Family. Nina smiled. Ever since she could remember, she'd wanted a family of her own. Was this her way of achieving one? Could she run an orphanage herself? Or better yet, adopt the children? Then, they truly would belong to her, and the more the merrier.

Steps lighter, she turned down another row of tents and grabbed the bucket she had stashed behind a pile of kindling. Extra buckets meant more water and keeping children clean was a never ending battle. She filled the bucket at the common area and, taking care not to spill any of the precious liquid, marched to her tent.

"I found another one," Johnny said the moment she arrived. His wire-haired mutt lay in the dirt at his feet. "The poor thing doesn't seem to have had a bite to eat for days."

That made five children under her care. She peeked into the tent to see a little girl around the age of five or six sitting cross-legged on a blanket. "Come on out, sweetie."

Wide-eyed, the child crawled from the tent.

Nina knelt in front of her. "What's your name?"

"Abby."

"Do you know where your parents are?"

"Under the house."

Tears sprang to Nina's eyes. She prayed that "under the house" meant they were safe in a basement, waiting to be found and released. "Do you know your surname?"

"Hayfield." She eyed the pot Johnny stirred.

"Johnny, when the stew is ready, give her all she wants. I'll eat later." Even though Nina had lost a few pounds, it wouldn't hurt her to skip a meal now and again in order to feed a child. "Right now, I need to post her name on the list of survivors in case her parents are looking for her. I'll be quick, so you can get to work."

"Yes, ma'am."

Nina headed for the camp entrance as quick as she could. She valued Johnny's help with the younger children, but didn't want to take advantage of his good will. He could manage well enough on his own and take little Sam with him.

A board stood just inside the entrance to the camp. Several sheets of paper were tacked to it, with the names of survivors looking to connect with their families. Nina's heart leaped to see several names crossed out with a thin line. That meant they had found their loved ones. A thick line meant they were among the dead.

"Nina!" Mabel hugged her. "Writing down another name, are you? You are a true angel of mercy."

"Just doing what God would ask of me." And filling a lonely hole in her heart at the same time.

"How many do you have now?"

"Counting Johnny and Sam, I have five."

"Five what?" Jacob approached from behind.

"Our dear, sweet Nina has been taking in orphans," Mabel volunteered.

"You share your tent with five children?" His face darkened.

Nina squared her shoulders, determined not to be intimidated. "Yes, I do. And I'll take in more as I find them until we're splitting the seams of the tent."

"Excuse us, Mrs. Stoltz." Jacob took Nina by the elbow

and pulled her a few feet away. "Are you aware of the dangers you have put yourself and those children in? Disease can spread like wildfire through a camp as crowded as this one."

"I'll take my chances." She jerked free. "I refuse to let them wander alone and afraid when I am capable of caring for them."

"But what if you can't?" He shook his head. "You've taken on a load of responsibility."

"I have a wonderful partner in God. We can handle the responsibility just fine."

"God does not always help."

She gasped. "What has happened in your past to make you so afraid of responsibility and of God?"

"I'm not afraid." He stiffened. "I just don't believe in taking on more than I can feasibly handle."

She blinked back tears at the pain she saw in his eyes. "We are each called to walk our own path through life, Jacob. This is mine." She headed back to her tent, allowing the tears she'd held to escape.

He seemed to carry such weight on his shoulders, such pain in his soul. While she wanted to cradle him against her as she would a child, she couldn't. Nor could she allow her feelings for him to grow further. She could not entangle her heart with the heart of a man so embittered against God as Jacob seemed to be. He might resemble the heroes she'd thought of earlier, but he was more of a black knight, content to wander the world alone.

No more would she follow after him. No more would she seek his help unless she had no other choice. The man seemed to want to exist alone behind the walls he'd built. She would respect that.

The moment she came within sight of her tent, Johnny called to his dog and dashed away, leaving his younger brother to play with the three other children, all under the age of ten. Compassion and love reared in Nina. How could she even consider sending them away? If the camp were to find a way to house the orphans, she would volunteer her services and accompany the children there. Until then, she would do what she could to lessen their burdens.

She cupped the cheek of each child she passed on her way to the pot hanging over the fire. She didn't need the love of a man. She would focus on giving love to the children. She sighed. Who was she kidding? She wanted a husband. She wanted Jacob. She didn't care that they'd only known each other for a little over a month. A disaster such as the one they shared brought out the truth in a person.

Johnny had left her a few bites of food, the dear boy. She pulled a spoon from her pocket and cleaned the pot. She could take the children with her to wash the dishes. The exercise would be good for them.

"Come along, children." Like a mother duck leading her young, she set off toward the common area in the center of the camp, which the refugees referred to as the park.

Jacob watched as Nina scraped the pot, then led her charges away from her tent. The silly woman wasn't getting enough to eat. Somehow, he needed to find more rations for her. If she insisted on taking in strays, he would help her from afar. No matter how he felt about her taking on such a burden, he cared for the stubborn woman and understood her desire to help. He only wished her helping didn't involve caring for so many.

Not wanting to invade her privacy, he still couldn't help but glance into her tent. Every square inch contained a pallet or thin mattress. The bed cots had been lifted on blocks of wood, allowing room underneath one for another sleeping area. The ground under the second cot contained

what little belongings the occupants owned. A few childish drawings were taped to the canvas walls. The tent was
clearly a home.

Jacob's heart melted a bit. Maybe Nina knew something he didn't.

Before completing his rounds, he filled her wash basin
and drinking water. He glanced to heaven, wanting to pray
for the safety of Nina and her charges, but afraid to pray
and not be heard. He sighed and headed for his lonely tent.

A gunshot sounded, causing him to switch direction
and race for the common area. Fear for Nina spurred him
faster.

He burst into the clearing just as Nina bashed a man
over the head with a cooking pot. Behind her cowered a
young Chinese girl.

"What's going on here?" Jacob stepped between
Nina and the man on the ground. He searched for a gun.
"Where's the gun?"

"I'm sorry, Sergeant." An older man stepped forward.
"I fired into the air in order to catch someone's attention.
It seems to have worked." He showed the pistol to Jacob.

"Put it away before you hurt someone." Jacob hauled
the man on the ground to his feet. "I'll repeat…what is
going on?"

"He accosted this girl." Nina raised the pot again.

Jacob took it from her and dropped it. He sighed. While
he believed prostitutes had rights, too, arresting a man approaching one would be tricky. "Did he harm you?" Keeping a firm grip on the man's arm, he peered around Nina.

The girl ducked her head further.

"He grabbed her and tried to kiss her." Nina planted
her fists on her hips. "I clearly heard her say no. When
he persisted, she screamed. Not one of these people were
willing to step forward and help, so I did." She lifted her

chin and glared at Jacob as if daring him to say something against her actions.

A few feet to the side of her huddled three children, wide eyes watching the proceedings. Jacob sighed again, knowing Nina had just added one more wounded bird to her flock. He turned to the man struggling to get away. "Sir, explain yourself."

"I was only wanting some company." He managed to yank free. "Why else would someone of her kind be here? There's a separate camp for the Chinese."

True. Why was the girl at the Golden Gate camp? A question for a later time. "Go home, sir. Nina, you, too."

"I need a new pot." She pointed at the dented one. "I expect that gentleman to provide one."

"For Pete's sake." The man grabbed a fairly new pot from the trough of water and threw it at Nina's feet.

"Hey!" Jacob narrowed his eyes. "One more move like that, and I'll have you arrested. Mind your manners around a lady or I'll mind them for you."

"Thank you." Nina picked up the pot, kicking the damaged one at the irate man, then took the Chinese girl's hand and led her and the rest of her brood away.

The woman wasn't safe washing dishes. Jacob shook his head and ordered everyone else to turn back to their chores and mind their own business.

"We can't have someone like that in our camp, sir." A plump woman called out. "She's a temptation to our men."

"Then I suggest you give your man no reason to be tempted." With those words, Jacob stormed off, trying to figure out what he intended to do with Nina's newest orphan. Yes, there was a separate camp designated for the Chinese, but suspicion told him the girl hadn't come to his camp soliciting business. She had come for sanctuary, most likely to escape her madam or the threat of violence.

He veered direction again and headed for Nina's tent.

The chatter of children came from inside, their forms silhouetted by the light of a lantern. Nina sat out front on a three-legged stool and poked at the dying embers of her cooking fire.

"I figured you would show up," she said, lifting her sad eyes to his. "I won't send her away."

"I'm not asking you to." He pulled up another stool. "I'm only asking that you take her in with your eyes open."

"Meaning I will meet with tough resistance from the other refugees?" She nodded. "She wants out, Jacob. I'll do everything I can to help her not return to that life."

"Even if it means endangering your life?" He knew her answer before she gave it, but needed her to know the truth of the situation.

"Yes. I have no family, other than what I create for myself. If I should perish doing good, then so be it." She squared her shoulders. "This is my calling in life…to help those like me."

So, she was an orphan, too. It all made sense to him now. Risking her wrath, he took her small hand in his. "My friendship is still here, should you want it."

Her eyes shimmered and she glanced down at their entwined fingers. "I accept. A girl can always use a friend. Especially during this tragedy."

His heart warmed at her acceptance. Under different circumstances, he could see himself in a relationship with the strong beauty, but a disaster such as they strove to overcome left no room for romance. Life was too uncertain for such attachments. He would cherish the little allowed them.

"I need to finish my rounds." He stood, letting her hand slip free and immediately missing the contact. "Please, let me know if I can be of service. Don't forget to sign up for extra rations. You're entitled to one for each member of your household."

"Others need it more and supplies are so scarce as it is."

"You can't care for these children if you succumb to illness, Nina." He reached down to cup her cheek, but then pulled back. Further contact with her would scorch him.

Her eyes widened. "I'm fine. Although, there is one thing."

"Anything." He would promise her the moon if it would make her smile.

"Surely, there is a pastor or two in the camp? Someone who can hold Sunday services? Matters of the soul cannot be cast aside, even in times such as these."

She was worried about church? Where was God when the earth shook? "I'll see what I can do."

As he headed for the far end of camp, he fought his resentment toward God. Not only for the death of his family, but for the prolonging of Jacob's enlistment time. He'd been so close, thought of little else during his morning walks on the beach. That morning of the earthquake had changed everything. He wanted the strong faith of Nina, but life had shown faith to be nothing more than a dream.

Lanterns were extinguished as he passed tents, the residents recognizing the mandatory lights out. The soft murmurs of mothers putting little ones to sleep, and the lower tones of fathers in conversation with their children tugged at him.

What would it be like to have a wife and family waiting for him at the end of the day? To have Nina waiting for him? He glanced through the darkening night, the horizon still lit by burning fires, toward Nina's tent. Was she telling bedtime stories to the children? Comforting the Chinese girl?

Or did she sit on the edge of her cot, brushing her long

golden hair while the soft snores of her charges filled the tent? Aware of the dangerous path his thoughts were taking, Jacob increased his pace until he arrived at his dark tent.

He shoved aside the flap. If church services would make Nina happy, he would search every corner of camp to find a pastor.

Chapter 7

"**I**'ve found your pastor."

Nina glanced up from cooking a simple breakfast of biscuits and a thin broth for gravy. "Really?" Hope leaped in her chest.

Jacob smiled and waved a man forward. "This is Pastor Herbert Collins."

He could not have given her a better gift. Nina wiped her hands on her apron and greeted the tall, well-dressed man. "I'm Nina Hansen, and I am very glad to make your acquaintance." Her hand fit perfectly in the man's thin one. While Mr. Collins did not have the striking physique and handsome features of Jacob, he was pleasant on the eyes. Kindness, and dare she say, admiration, shined from his eyes.

"The pleasure is all mine, Miss Hansen." He gave her hand a quick shake before releasing it. "The kind sergeant has informed me you are wanting Sunday services?"

"Yes, please." There may very well be services held already in the camp, but if so, she had yet to hear of one.

"I also hear you've been taking in strays," Mr. Collins said.

"Oh, yes. Being an orphan myself, I have always been on the lookout for a family of my own, if only a temporary one." Her face heated. Why was she telling this stranger her personal history? Her desire for a family was her business and no one else's.

Jacob's face paled. No doubt he thought her silly to babble on the way she was. Well, although he seemed to have no desire to include anyone else in his personal world, she was different. She would befriend or mother anyone God put in her path to care for.

"I may need help spreading the word." Mr. Collins beamed at her. "Would you have time in your busy schedule to assist me?"

Jacob's face darkened. My, the man's complexion changed shades faster than the fire spreading through the city.

"I would love to." She placed a hand on Jacob's arm. "Jacob will assist, too, won't you?"

"Of course." The words sounded strangled, as if he had to force them from his throat.

Nina bit back a giggle. She would soften the sergeant's heart if she had anything to say about it. If they worked together, he'd have no choice but to spend time with her and the children.

"Wonderful." Mr. Collins rubbed his hands together. "I'll be by this afternoon and we can discuss the details."

"Why not stop by for dinner?" Nina glanced from one man to the other. "You, too, Jacob."

He shook his head. "You have so many to feed now. You don't need an extra at your cooking fire."

"There is always enough for you. Please say you'll return." She stood on tiptoe and placed a gentle kiss on his cheek. "Thank you."

Jacob gave a curt nod, high spots of color blooming on his cheeks, then whirled on his well-shined military boots and marched away. Nina shrugged. She didn't have time to try and figure out why he seemed displeased. If it was because she had another mouth to feed, he'd stated his opinion plenty of times. This was her business.

She had only issued an invitation to dinner, and a simple one at that. Not a marriage proposal. She put her hand over her lips. He couldn't be upset over a chaste kiss, could he?

She transferred her attention to the still-grinning Mr. Collins. "Well, I'm sure you have things to tend to."

"Not really." He rocked on his heels. "Normally, my days are filled with helping the lost and hurting." His gaze drifted to the tent entrance where Orchid, Nina's newest charge, peered out. "But, I see you have your own to tend to. I offer you my services."

Nina studied his face, waiting for the same hungry expectation that crossed the features of many of the other men who caught sight of the beautiful Chinese girl. When she didn't see even a glimmer, she smiled. "We're doing fine, for now, but your offer is appreciated. I will also ask that you keep Orchid's whereabouts to yourself."

"Of course." He nodded. "Nothing good can come of people knowing where she's staying."

Nina smiled. Perhaps she had found a kindred spirit. Friend or not, though, Mr. Collins needed to be on his way so she could tend to the children. She kept the smile on her lips and stood silently until he took her hint.

"Until dinner, Miss Hansen." He turned and strolled down the row of tents, calling out greetings to others who prepared their morning meal.

What on earth would she serve for dinner? While the children ate, Orchid choosing to take hers inside the tent, Nina mentally went through their meager supplies. A few cans of stew, some flour. It would have to do.

She eyed her camera. It had been days since the opportunity to record history had presented itself. While the fires were out, the city still lay in ruins. Oh, the stories to be told outside the camp's perimeter, and inside. She glanced down the row of tents flapping in the breeze, each makeshift home exactly like the one beside it. She grabbed her camera and snapped a picture.

Thanks to a kindhearted reporter of an eastern newspaper, she had plenty of film and a few dollars in her pocket by way of the postal service, which was working again. They were paying for her photos, something she had only ever dreamed of.

Torn between the desire to pursue her dream and to care for the children, Nina remained in the row between tents. What was going on at the beach? Were the soldiers back at the fort? So many historical events to be captured.

"Orchid?"

She poked her head out of the tent and nodded. Other than her name, Nina had not been able to get the girl to say a word.

"Might I trouble you to watch the little ones?"

Orchid nodded, dashed out and ushered the children inside, then closed the flap.

"I won't be gone long. I promise." Her steps lighter than they had been in days, Nina fairly skipped the few blocks to the ocean, snapping pictures of people going about their new daily routines. An hour a day. That's all she would give herself to snap photographs. It would be enough.

Waves crashed against the shore. Nina removed her shoes, and stepped into the surf. Her laughter rang out, startling seagulls. She snapped a photo as they surged as one into a startlingly blue sky. Behind her lay a blackened city, before her was the proof that beauty still existed. She closed her eyes and lifted her face to the sun.

She sensed someone behind her, and turned. Jacob, shoes in hand, stepped into the shallow surf.

"Hello, again," he said.

"Are you following me?" Dare she hope he was?

"I did see you coming this way, yes." He gave her a small smile. "This is always a favorite place of mine to come when I have a spare moment. It's a great place to think."

She fought back a frown. So, he hadn't exactly come with a desire to spend time with her. "I've always loved the ocean." She turned back to the water. She wouldn't dwell on the pain that came with knowing he hadn't sought her out. "You must have quite a lot to think about, being in charge of the camp and all."

"Yes. My enlistment time is almost up. I've already extended it once, by request of my commanding officer and on account of the disaster."

Nina dug her toes into the damp sand. "You'll be leaving, then?"

"I haven't decided. San Francisco is my home now. There is no ocean in Kansas."

Kansas. So far. Her heart fell. What would she do if he were to leave? Not that they could be anything more than friends. Not with the way Jacob felt about her faith, but her heart refused to follow her mind.

"I should be getting back," she said. "I promised Orchid I wouldn't be gone more than an hour."

"You also shouldn't be wandering alone. It isn't safe."

She stared into his worried face. "Don't you ever do things just because it feels right?"

"I don't understand."

Of course he wouldn't. Jacob saw things in black and white.

"A girl needs time alone with God. That isn't something I can get much of in a crowded camp."

"God? I found you a pastor."

Nina shook her head and dropped to the sand, unmindful of her skirt, and slipped her feet back into her shoes. She'd been a fool to hope for more than friendship from Jacob. Clearly his heart was not in San Francisco.

Jacob changed to a clean uniform in preparation for dinner. On the overturned crate he used as a nightstand sat a tin of shortbread cookies. He wasn't sure why he had accepted Nina's invitation, other than he hated to eat alone, and wanted to spend time with her when he wasn't barking orders. Since he had decided to go, he didn't want to arrive empty-handed. Nina had enough trouble feeding her brood without him eating her meager supplies.

As ready as he would be, he tucked the cookies under his arm and set off for the other side of camp. Mr. Collins seemingly appeared out of nowhere and fell into step with him. What in the world would they talk about? Jacob hoped the man wouldn't use the opportunity to preach. If he did, Jacob would have to cut his visit short.

It wasn't that he didn't believe in God, he did. He just didn't have time for a god that would take the lives of innocent people.

"Good evening, Sergeant." Mr. Collins smiled. "I see you've brought dessert. I managed to get my hands on some canned milk and peaches for the little ones."

"A windfall for sure." Jacob eyed the dent-free cans. While supplies were arriving from neighboring states, they usually looked beat up by the time they arrived at the camp. Mr. Collins's cans looked remarkably new.

"What do you think of the little Chinese gal in Miss Hansen's care?" Mr. Collins rubbed his chin. "If she is a former prostitute from Chinatown, there could be unfavorable repercussions for Miss Hansen. Not only could her reputation be marred, but those who claim the girl as their property wouldn't stop at violence to retrieve her."

"I've thought of that, but our dear Miss Hansen is stubborn and refuses to listen to reason." Jacob squared his shoulders. He wanted to ask whether the pastor had set his cap for Nina, but held his tongue. It was none of his concern who courted her. Someone needed to convince his heart of the fact.

"I wonder why the lovely woman is not married." Mr. Collins took a deep breath through his nose and straightened the tie at his throat.

Yes, the man definitely seemed to have thoughts of courtship on his mind. The thought rankled, despite Jacob's reluctance to marry. Marriage brought responsibility for others, not something he desired. Still, here he was, responsible for thousands. Now, if he could find a place where disaster could never strike or illness could never kill, he might consider taking a bride. Since those places didn't exist on earth, he would remain a bachelor.

Nina's tent came into view, and he quickened his steps. How would he get through dinner with a bore such as Mr. Collins, especially if the man regaled Nina with flowery speech? Not that he knew the man well, but he did seem a bit of a stuffed shirt in Jacob's opinion.

Nina looked lovely in a spotless white shirtwaist and navy skirt. While it was the same sort of attire she wore every day, she had piled her hair high on her head and greeted them with a smile. The setting sun cast a halo around her blond head, making her look like an angel. Jacob's mouth dried.

"Welcome, gentlemen." She kept her hands folded demurely in front of her. "The children have already eaten, so we will be able to discuss our business in peace. I hope stew is sufficient for our meal."

"More than so, Miss Hansen." Mr. Collins handed her his offering. "A thank-you gift for inviting me."

"I brought dessert." Jacob thrust the tin of cookies at her.

Her eyes widened as she graciously accepted both gifts. "You gentlemen are too kind. Please sit." She waved a hand graciously to two of three stools. "I'll serve our meal and we can discuss the church services after we eat."

Jacob's shoulders slumped. He had forgotten the real reason for the dinner invitation. They were gathered to discuss when, and where, to hold the first church service. He would most likely be expected to attend, too. Why had he allowed himself to be swayed by a pretty face?

After dishing out three bowls of stew, Nina turned to Mr. Collins. "Would you say the blessing, please?"

"I'd be delighted."

Jacob bowed his head out of courtesy and thought of his long list of chores he needed to attend to before retiring for the night. If their religious planning took too long, he would have to excuse himself. He almost hoped it would take a while to eat, so as to cut into the planning time.

Alas, it was not to be. Nina rushed them through their meal, stacked the dirty bowls beside the fire pit and clapped her hands. "Let's get started. Mr. Collins, I suggest we hold the services in a corner of the common area each Sunday at 10 a.m."

"I couldn't agree more, Miss Hansen." He stretched his legs in front of him and crossed them at the ankles. "There are other pastors in the camp, but it won't be difficult to find a place where they don't preach."

She looked startled. "There are already services being held?" She glanced at Jacob. "I haven't heard of any."

He shrugged, hoping she would forgive him for not letting her know. He had wanted to fulfill her simple request himself. "It is my understanding that they are not consistent."

"Oh." She looked at the pastor. "I pray you will be, Mr. Collins?"

"As faithful as the sun's rising." He folded his arms across his middle. "God's children need consistent feeding, don't you agree, Sergeant?"

Jacob wanted to strangle the pompous man. Of course, the man would agree with anything Nina said. He felt as if she could say the sky was green and the pastor would agree. "Most definitely."

"Do you have any particular subjects you feel led to teach on?" Nina asked. The eyes that could convince Jacob to do almost anything, despite his reluctance, focused on Mr. Collins.

"My main idea is to encourage others to turn to our Heavenly Father during this time of tribulation. I would like to help them see that He hasn't forgotten them."

Nina beamed. "Exactly. Don't you think so, Jacob?"

What he thought was that they shouldn't be in such dire straits to begin with, but instead said, "I suppose."

"Jacob struggles a bit with knowing a loving God," Nina explained. "We'll have to help him past that."

Mr. Collins gave him a pitying look. "How unfortunate."

Enough was enough. Jacob stood. "Dinner was delicious, Nina, but I have things to tend to before lights out." He marched away.

His thoughts tumbled, similar to the time he'd turned his back on the sea and been rolled by a wave. Despite his resolve to never settle down, jealousy reared its ugly head. Maybe he should have stayed instead of leaving the pastor alone with Nina. He had practically served her to the man on a platter!

"Wedding rings for sale, soldier." A wiry elderly man held out a wooden box. "A strapping man such as yourself can have your pick of the ladies. Marriage is a hot commodity right now."

Jacob whirled in the other direction. Everywhere he went he was slapped in the face by others finding their life's mate. Maybe he should consider heading home to Kansas at the end of his enlistment. Maybe people were more levelheaded there.

The night seemed quiet. No gunshots or drunken brawls. No one wandering the camp after dark.

While he wasn't the only military man keeping order in the camp, he did seem to be the one who patrolled the most. What would the residents do if Jacob left? Would pandemonium be the norm or would the rules that Jacob put into place continue?

Yes, it would be time to leave soon. He was getting ensnared by the people he was assigned to oversee, and in danger of moving away from his promise of not getting too involved in other people's lives. In particular, the life of one lovely Nina Hansen and the children she cared for.

Rounds complete, Jacob strolled by Nina's tent, relieved to see that Collins was gone. A lamp burned inside. Nina's soft murmurs drifted through the canvas as she most likely took the young ones through their nightly routines. He wished it were possible to find a larger tent for her. He'd heard rumors of temporary homes that the refugees could soon rent. If Nina had the means of making an income, the new housing might be a solution.

He continued to his own tent and disrobed, placing his uniform neatly across the back of a chair. He paid a woman to do his laundry, but still did his best to wear his uniforms several times before washing.

He lay on his back on his cot, arms folded under his head, and pondered his lonely future. While he loved San Francisco, even in the city's current condition, he wasn't sure he could stay after retiring. The life of a Kansas farmer might be exactly what his weary soul needed.

If only he could honestly contemplate never seeing Nina again. That particular thought ripped at his heart.

He couldn't deny it. He was in a dilemma.

Chapter 8

Nina shuddered as Johnny's dog bit into yet another rat. While the boy and his dog made a fair bit of change by turning in the dead rats to the army, it seemed a rather gruesome way of making money. She snapped a photo of Johnny holding up his wiggling, bulging bag. The daily hour she allotted for taking photographs was almost up and, while she enjoyed spending time with the brave fifteen-year-old, she yearned to head into the city and photograph the work being done.

The fires had been put out weeks ago. The newspapers back east would love to see what, if any, progress was being made in the once great city of San Francisco. The residents of the camp seemed to have adjusted to life in the refugee camp. Their strength and fortitude to rebuild must surely show progress in the burned and fallen areas, as well.

"Do you need more photographs, Miss Hansen?" Johnny's question pulled her out of her thoughts. "A group of boys are gathering in the common area to play ball."

"I've finished." She hung her camera around her neck. "Run and play."

She spotted Jacob on patrol as he headed to the camp's entrance. Here was her chance to venture into the city. She quickened her pace and caught up with him as he passed the entrance.

"Where are you going? May I accompany you?" From the look on his face, he wanted to say no. She pasted on her most beguiling smile. "The fires are out, and the dynamiting has stopped, weeks have passed since the quake. The danger must be at a very minimum."

"I'm headed to the base, and no, you may not. There is still looting and fighting." He crossed his hands behind his back and kept walking.

At least he hadn't said no. "I have a market back east and the newspapers are paying me for photographs. I really would like to take some of the reconstruction."

"We won't be doing much more than cleanup for a very long time."

"Then I'll photograph those efforts." She hurried to keep up with his long strides. "I'll be perfectly safe with you."

He sighed and nodded. "Fine, but you must obey me immediately if I give you an order."

"Yes, sir!" She saluted, her grin widening. A morning spent with Jacob definitely made the top of her list of things she enjoyed.

The odor of scorched wood greeted them almost instantly. Large groups of men tossed bricks and boards into the backs of wagons, stopping to watch as Jacob and Nina passed. She snapped photographs as quickly as she could, not wanting Jacob to get too far ahead and have a reason to scold.

"Must you stop every two seconds?" he asked. "It will take us forever."

"Where are we going?"

"To see my supervisor." He kept his face forward, a muscle ticking in his jaw. "My time is almost up, and I need to let him know that I do not intend to reenlist."

Her heart squeezed. So, he was leaving. She might as

well resign herself to the fact there could definitely be nothing between them. If she wanted a husband to go along with her ready-made family, she would have to look elsewhere.

Maybe this was God's sign she was meant to remain unmarried. Would He keep her heart's desire from coming true? She hid her tearing eyes behind the camera and snapped Jacob's profile. This photo she would keep for herself.

They entered a hastily erected building. "Stay here." Jacob pointed to a hard-backed chair and stepped through another door.

Nina eyed her sparse surroundings. Several "Wanted!" posters adorned the otherwise empty walls. Not having ever spotted the men pictured, she turned to peer at a nearby desk. A few papers, maps, mostly, littered the battered surface. Boredom soon set in, and she hoped for Jacob's quick return.

Half an hour later, he joined her, high spots of color on his cheeks, and quickly led her from the building. She wanted to ask him how his meeting had gone, but his stony face answered her question.

"Do you want to take a quick walk on the beach?" Anything to return a smile to his face.

He nodded, and changed direction.

On the beach, they removed their shoes and stepped to the water's edge. Without speaking, Nina slipped her hand into Jacob's. He glanced at her in surprise, then entwined his fingers with hers. In silence, they watched the waves kiss the sand.

As each wave lapped at their feet, Jacob's tension seemed to ease. Nina smiled. Yes, she could be his friend, if nothing else, for the time allotted to her. "Let's walk."

They strolled along the wet sand, seagulls crying over

their heads. It was easy to forget a city lay in ruins behind them or that children waited for Nina's return. "As much as I would enjoy doing this all day, I must get back. I feel guilty leaving the children in Orchid's care."

"How is she doing?"

"She still won't speak to me, although I've heard her whispering to the little ones. Her English is very good."

"Give her time. She's wounded. I'll see what my commanding officer recommends the next time I see him."

When they reached the camp, Jacob placed a soft kiss on her cheek, leaving her face heated. She would always feel his lips against her skin. "Thank you. I needed the walk."

She swallowed the lump in her throat. "Maybe we could do it daily. Until you leave."

"Yes, I would like that." He smiled and left with her heart in his calloused hands.

"Miss Hansen." Mr. Collins hurried toward her. "I didn't have the opportunity to speak with you after last Sunday's service. I hope it met with your approval."

Nina shoved aside her sadness and forced a smile. The friendly man seemed to be wherever she was, more times than not. "Very much. The topic of handing over tough situations to God was very timely."

"Thank you, but there is a more pressing reason for seeking you out." He glanced around them.

"Oh?"

"There is a Chinese gentleman asking questions around camp about a missing girl. I believe he means your Orchid. I fear he may intend her harm."

Nina clutched the ribbon around her neck. "Does he suspect where she is?"

"I do not believe so." He bent closer to her. "I suspect your girl might be a highly sought-after prostitute. You could be in danger by housing her."

While he was most likely correct, Nina had no intentions of telling Orchid to leave. "Please do not mention this to Sergeant Taft." Jacob would force Nina to send the girl away.

"I have a small store of supplies," Mr. Collins said. "If you are not opposed to the idea, I will bring them to your tent and take most of my meals with you. The presence of a man might discourage anyone from causing harm."

"That is kind of you. Thank you. Since it appears we will be spending quite a bit of time together, please call me Nina." She glanced to where Jacob had gone. Was this God's sign that she had been looking for a soul mate in the wrong place?

"And I am Herbert." He linked his arm, inviting her to slip her hand into the crook of his elbow. "We are coconspirators for the good of mankind."

Nina giggled. "It's time for me to head back. I'd like to take the children to the assigned play area. We call it the park. You are welcome to come along."

Soon, minus Orchid, Nina and Herbert ushered Sam and the younger children to a corner of the park where they immediately plopped into a sandpit and began to build, Sam stating they were going to rebuild San Francisco.

Nina laughed as she sat and reclined back on her hands, letting the sun warm her face. She tuned out Herbert's chatter, the man did like the sound of his own voice, and thought of Jacob's kiss. How silly she was. The gesture had been nothing more than what a man might give his sister, yet it had sent butterflies dancing in her stomach.

Wait. Had Herbert stopped talking? Nina opened her eyes. Clearly, he had said something to which she needed to respond. "Excuse me?"

"You seem miles away." He offered a shaky smile. "What are you thinking of, if you don't mind my asking?"

She couldn't very well tell him the truth. "Oh, well…" She was saved by cries from her youngest, who had gotten sand in her eyes. "Here, sweetheart." She wiped Abby's eyes with the hem of her skirt. "You're okay. No throwing dirt, all right?"

Abby nodded and continued to play.

"You're a natural mother," Herbert said. "It's a wonder you haven't married."

"My life has been full with the orphanage. There hasn't been time."

He leaned closer. "I hope you will someday reconsider." Oh, dear.

"There's the man I told you about." Herbert pointed to a large Chinese man watching their group from the shade of a tree.

The man's cold stare sent shivers of dread down Nina's spine. Did he know for a fact that she harbored Orchid or was he merely searching? Either way, Nina needed to find a safer place for the young girl to live.

After breaking up yet another fight over water, Jacob headed to the common ground. Many of the refugees gathered there each day. Too many people in one place often resulted in disagreements that sometimes turned ugly. He hoped it wasn't so today. After the type of morning he'd had, he could welcome a bit of peaceful tranquility among the masses.

He stood in the shade and watched a man who seemed to be spying on someone. The man's dark, braided hair hung to his waist. His muscles strained the silk fabric of his spotless white *hanfu*. Every inch of him shouted danger.

Jacob followed his gaze. The Chinese man's stare was fixated on Nina and Mr. Collins.

Dread twanged Jacob's nerves. He hurried to Nina's

side. "Gather up the children. It's time for you to head back to your tent."

She nodded, glanced over his shoulder and called to the young ones who scampered to her side. Once they were close, she and Mr. Collins herded them off the grassy area and disappeared among the tents.

Jacob continued to watch the Chinese man until he whirled, his queue flying, and marched in the other direction. If the man was after Orchid, and knew where Nina lived, she and the children were in danger. He rubbed his chin. Perhaps, he could have Nina switch tents with someone who lived closer to Jacob. Although Mr. Collins seemed permanently attached to Nina's hip, Jacob would sleep better knowing she was closer to his own tent.

His commanding officer had agreed, in writing, that Jacob's term would end in a month. He needed to erase the danger to Nina before he left.

Jacob turned toward Nina's tent to present his plan. If she said no, he would press the issue. Mr. Collins didn't look the type of man to be able to stand up to a physical threat. Verbally, however, the man could talk the beak off a seagull.

Jacob frowned at the sight of the pastor whispering in Nina's ear. Something like jealousy rose in him, but that couldn't be it. Why should Jacob care if Nina found a man other than him to care for her?

He knew why. His military time was running out and, if he were honest and wanted to take a wife, he wanted one like Nina.

Would she love Kansas? Could a city girl be happy in a rural area where the nearest neighbor was miles away?

Nina glanced up and stepped away from Mr. Collins. "Thank you for coming to our aid, Jacob, although I don't think the man meant us any harm."

"Don't be ridiculous. Of course he did." Jacob spoke sharper than he had intended, immediately regretting his words at the wounded expression on Nina's face. "I'd like you and the children to move to a tent closer to mine. I'm sure I can find someone willing to trade with you, and I'm sure Mr. Collins will help you move."

"Surely it isn't as dangerous as you make it out to be." Nina moved in front of her tent entrance as if to shelter those inside. "Maybe the man is a relative of Orchid's."

"I have no relatives." Orchid stepped outside. "This man wants to take me back. He is very bad. I must leave."

"No." Nina put an arm around her shoulders. "Jacob, do something."

He rubbed the area between his eyes as a headache threatened. "I will speak with my supervisor and see if there is a safer place for her."

"Thank you." The smile on Nina's face tempted Jacob to fulfill her every wish.

Hoping he hadn't spoken too soon, he said his good-byes with a promise to return later, and headed to the base. He found Captain Walker sitting down for his evening meal.

"Permission to speak, sir." Jacob stood at attention.

"Relax, soldier." The captain straightened in his chair. "Please don't tell me you're backing out of extending your enlistment another month. You're sorely needed."

"No, sir." Jacob sat in the chair opposite the captain. The army wouldn't discharge him early anyway unless he was incapable of fulfilling his duties. "One of the refugees is harboring a young Chinese girl, believed to be a highly sought-after prostitute. I believe her location has been discovered and the girl, and the kind woman who took her in, are in danger."

"Have her send the girl away."

"I was hoping you knew of another alternative, sir." Nina would never send Orchid away.

The captain sighed. "Don't think me unfeeling, Sergeant, but the plight of a prostitute does not take precedence over the million other things on my mind."

"Could we send her to the base?"

"And have her tempt every soldier barracked here? No."

"Is there anywhere she can go?" He didn't want to tell Nina he had failed her.

The captain tapped his fork on the side of his plate. "There is an older woman who takes in such girls. She lives in one of the few sections of the city spared from the fires. You can check to see whether she has room. Her name is Mrs. Redmond." He scribbled an address on a slip of paper and handed it to Jacob. "Good luck."

"Thank you, sir." Jacob stood and took his leave, heading to the far edge of the city to the Mission San Francisco de Asis section.

The fires had practically licked at the woman's doorstep having stopped one street over. Jacob maneuvered around the wreckage and made his way to a small clapboard house, its white paint now a dingy gray from layers of soot. He lifted the door knocker and let it fall.

A woman easily six feet tall and as thin as she was tall opened the door. "How may I help you, soldier?"

"I've heard you take in…uh, a certain type of ladies?" His neck heated.

She stiffened. "If you've come looking for entertainment, sir, you may march away. This is not that type of house."

"No, ma'am, begging your pardon. Captain Walker said you may have room for one more? A friend of mine has taken in a young girl, and I fear for my friend's safety."

Mrs. Redmond clamped her lips together, spearing him

with a gray-eyed gaze. "There have been others here searching for a girl called Orchid. Is this who you speak of?"

He nodded. "Since they've already been here, perhaps they won't come again."

"I'm not sure I can take that chance. These girls have been through so much already." She glanced over her shoulder, then stepped onto the porch, closing the door behind her. "I cannot put them in danger. The girl with your friend is important to the man in charge of the Chinese underground. These are very dangerous people."

"Please. My friend has some young ones in her care, also."

"Have this friend of yours come speak with me." Mrs. Redmond entered the house, leaving Jacob standing alone. He wondered whether the woman thought him dishonest.

By the time he returned to Nina, the sun was setting. Whatever she cooked over her fire set his stomach to rumbling, reminding him he hadn't eaten since breakfast.

"Come and eat, Jacob," she said with a smile.

He glanced around for Mr. Collins, overly pleased that the man was nowhere in sight. "Thank you. I'm starved."

She plopped a pile of beans in the center of a tin plate and handed it to him. "Tell me how your conversation went."

He recounted his conversation with Captain Walker, and then his visit with Mrs. Redmond. As he spoke, Nina's features grew stubborn. "So, she wants to meet you."

"I don't see what meeting me has to do with anything." Nina put a lid on the pot and removed it from the fire. "Either she wants to help or not. Besides, I think Orchid staying there may be too dangerous."

"More dangerous than her staying here?"

Nina shrugged. "I'll reserve judgment until I've spoken with the woman."

"Why are you so stubborn?"

"Why do you care?" She bolted to her feet. "You're leaving us just when we need you the most. If not for Mr. Collins, I don't know what I'd do."

Him again. "I'm doing everything I can." Jacob ran his fingers through his hair. "I care about you, Nina. You and the kids, as surprising as that may seem to you, and this is the best solution I could come up with."

"You care for me?" A smile teased at her lips. "Enough to continue joining me for Sunday services?"

"What does church have to do with anything?"

"It isn't really church that matters, Jacob. It's your relationship with God. I can't be unevenly yoked."

What in the world was she talking about? "Why do so many of our conversations come back to God?"

"Because it's important to me." She planted fists on her hips.

For goodness sake. "I'll return in the morning to escort you to Mrs. Redmond's."

"Thank you." She grinned. "I have another woman living here now, and my tent is crowded."

Jacob sighed and glanced at the sky.

Chapter 9

With Orchid dressed in Nina's extra set of clothes, and a wide-brimmed hat hiding her face and dark hair, Nina waited for Jacob. Her gaze returned time and again to the space between the tents. There he was.

She stepped forward to greet him. "We're ready."

He eyed Orchid. "We don't know for sure that Mrs. Redmond will take her in."

"She'll have to." Nina folded her hands tight enough to cause her nails to dig into her palms. "I heard footsteps outside our tent last night. I fear for her safety."

Jacob nodded. "Let's make haste." Keeping Orchid between him and Nina, he led them into the streets of San Francisco.

They passed military vehicles laden with supplies. Tears sprang to Nina's eyes. The rest of the nation was coming to their aid. The citizens of San Francisco would be all right. She grinned at Jacob over Orchid's head, his returning smile sending her heart somersaulting.

At Tenth Avenue and Fulton Street, they stopped to watch trick cyclists, a skit, and a one-act Carmen show in front of the damaged Opera House. After pausing for a few minutes to watch the entertainment, Jacob led them on.

An Italian woman sat on a pile of bricks while holding a

wailing infant. She glanced up, pointing at her chest. "No milk since ground shake."

Another woman, her hair as red as the bricks the mother sat on, plopped a child into the dirt and held out her arms. "I've enough milk for two."

Nina choked back a sob at the kindness of strangers. Jacob reached around Orchid and patted her shoulder as cars from other cities passed, signs painted on their sides declaring they were from Los Angeles, Burlington, Iowa, Buffalo, New York. So strong was her relief, Nina's knees sagged. Despite her faith, she had begun to think they'd been deserted. "God is with us."

"Aid has been arriving since a week after the quake," Jacob said. He stepped to her side and put an arm around her waist. "That's how we've been able to feed all the refugees."

She glanced up into his face, his gesture of comfort bringing tears to her eyes. "God has not deserted His people. Surely you can see that now."

His eyes twinkled. "I'm beginning to. I've even heard the Barnum and Bailey Circus contributed a day's receipts in the amount of twenty thousand dollars. It's hard not to see something, or someone, larger at work here."

"I'm glad to hear that." Nina put her hand over his. Maybe there was a future for the two of them after all. "Let's make sure Orchid is safe and then take our walk on the beach. We've neglected that over the last few days."

His smile broadened. "Let's hurry, then." He continued to talk as they walked, regaling her of other tales of America's kindness. Trainloads of clothing had arrived. The Salvation Army women had stood on the corners of New York and raised over one hundred and eighty-five thousand dollars. The great city of Chicago had held benefits to help the refugees. "And those are only the stories I've heard," he said.

As he spoke, tears coursed down Nina's face. How could she have ever doubted?

Although Jacob had removed his arm and returned to Orchid's other side, the strength in his touch had given Nina what she needed to continue hoping. She lifted her ever-present camera and snapped photographs: two men sitting at a table draped with a white tablecloth, eating from cans. Soldiers indulging in a bit of horseplay next to a long bread line. Others digging through rubble for survivors. Life went on in all its joy, misery and humor. Nina felt blessed to be included, despite the horror of the earthquake.

"We're here." Jacob approached the door of a nondescript house and knocked.

A tall woman answered, took one look at Orchid and ushered them inside. "I thought you had changed your mind."

"This is Nina Hansen," Jacob introduced, "and this is Orchid."

Orchid removed her hat and met the woman's gaze. "I very much want to stay here. I have heard you help girls like me."

The woman sighed. "I've heard of you, too. You've caused quite a ruckus by running off. I hope I don't regret changing my mind to help you, but God placed it on my heart years ago to be of service to those who want to leave that life." She crossed her arms. "Not only are the Chinese after you. There's a white man who would love to get you in his clutches, too, from what I've heard. But I think you'll be safe here. At least, I'm prepared to face any danger you may bring with you. May she keep the clothes, Miss Hansen?"

"Of course." Nina would see about replacing them from the stores arriving on the train. "Thank you. I'm staying at the Golden Gate Refugee Camp. Please let me know if you need anything." She turned to Orchid. "I will come and visit you the moment I feel it is safe." She wrapped the girl in a hug.

Orchid nodded, the glimmer of a smile appearing on her lips. "Thank you for rescuing me."

Nina hugged her again and followed Jacob outside. "I can't thank you enough."

"I didn't do it only for her." His eyes darkened as he glanced at her and cupped her cheek. "Surely, you know I would do anything in my power for you."

Her heart skipped a beat. Words failed at the heated look in his eyes. For a moment, she thought he would kiss her. For that moment, she desperately wanted him to.

Cries of alarm separated them, and Jacob whirled, pulling his pistol from its holster. He let out a breath upon discovering it was just the soldiers continuing to play, the "cry" a woman's flirtatious glee. Still, the moment of tenderness Nina and Jacob had shared was gone.

She forced a smile. "To the beach?"

He crooked his arm. "The highlight of my day."

The beach was anything but tranquil when they arrived. Ferries full of supplies docked at a newly repaired wharf, and men scurried to and fro unloading crates. One of the crates fell, busting open and spilling clothing across the sand. Nina glanced at Jacob.

He laughed. "Go and replace your skirt. Get something for the children, too."

Nina dashed forward, filling her arms with a clean, but used brown skirt and pale yellow blouse, pants for the boys and dresses for the girls. It was like Christmas.

She laughed and thrust her treasures into Jacob's hands. "Be a gentleman and carry these for me."

He bowed. "Your wish is my command."

Again, hope for their future leaped within her and then faded just as quickly. Joy filled her that he seemed to be softening toward God, but despair that he would be leaving in a few weeks threatened to overtake her happiness. A cloud passed over the sun, mirroring her sudden change of mood.

"I need to get back and relieve Johnny of his babysitting duties." She marched across the sand.

He jogged to catch up with her. "Tell me of the new woman living with you."

A safe subject, sort of, and one that wouldn't tear at her emotions. "Her name is Mary Southards. I found her living under a tree in the common area. Since the camp is full, and there was nowhere for her to go, I took her in."

"Why doesn't she watch the children when you accompany me?"

A good question, and one that Nina wouldn't mind hearing the answer to. "She seems to be gone a good part of the time, only returning to eat and sleep. But, she's a grown woman and does contribute to our supplies, so I have no reason to complain."

"As long as she doesn't pose a threat to you or the children."

"I don't think she does." Nina touched his arm. "Come for dinner and meet her for yourself."

"I will. Thank you."

Now all she needed to do was find something other than stew to prepare and to make Mary presentable. Her hair was matted and her clothes dirty and torn. She hadn't done anything to correct a person's first impression of a vagabond. If Jacob were to see her in her current state, he would shout danger for sure.

How could Jacob convince Nina to stop bringing stray refugees to her tent? While he admired her kindness, loved her for it, in fact, she was only putting her and the children at the risk of disease and starvation. Plus, there was Johnny's thrill at catching rats. The vermin carried all sorts of diseases. While Jacob couldn't fault the boy for wanting to make a few coins, he did wish the boy wouldn't bring the bag of dead rodents to Nina's tent before disposing of them. He was pretty sure she didn't crave seeing how many he had killed.

He scraped the razor along his jaw. Whether he courted Nina or not, she held a large part of his heart. The horror of the earthquake would be small in comparison to the danger to his mind and heart if he couldn't keep her safe.

Face smooth, he wiped the cream off on a towel and donned his uniform. Three more weeks until he was a civilian again. Excitement was shadowed by his indecision as to where to go from there. Stay in San Francisco or head home to Kansas. If not for Nina, his decision would be an easy one.

He walked to Nina's tent, keeping a close watch on the happenings around camp. For the most part, things ran smoothly every day. He broke up any fights, which thankfully were few and far between, put out cooking fires too close to tents and searched for the occasional lost child. But, despite the seemingly smooth running, he felt there were dirty dealings being run in the shadows. Those were what kept him patrolling late each evening.

He frowned, seeing Herbert Collins once again at Nina's fire. Did the man ever leave? Another box of food sat at the man's feet. Jacob shook his head. He'd completely forgotten to bring anything to add to the meal.

"Good evening, Nina. Mr. Collins." Jacob sat in a vacant chair.

"No need for formality, Sergeant. Herbert is my name. May I call you Jacob?" He grinned.

Jacob wanted to say no, not having a desire to form a friendship with the man. Instead, he nodded and glanced around for the elusive Mary.

"She's in the tent," Nina said, filling a plate with rice and canned meat. "She'll be out in a moment."

Seconds later, a small mouse of a woman in clean, but patched clothing, emerged from the tent. She cast a timid glance Jacob's way, giving the impression she might run and hide if he were to make a sudden move.

"Jacob, Herbert, this is Mary." Nina handed the woman a plate.

Both men nodded, Herbert sizing her up as if she were a prize cow to be sold at auction. Jacob snorted and focused on his food. There was something about Herbert Collins that didn't ring true. No one could smile that much all the time or seem so happy every minute of the day. Even good-natured Nina had her moments of sadness or annoyance. Usually directed at something Jacob did.

He smiled, thinking of the times they had clashed in differences of opinion. Nina might have a heart as big as the state of California, but she was also as stubborn as any woman he'd ever met. He didn't want her any other way, but he couldn't help noticing how even-tempered she was around Herbert. Maybe Jacob was the only one who brought out the fire in Nina.

"Share the humor, Jacob." Nina returned his smile.

He shook his head. If he were to admit to how much he enjoyed their disagreements, they might have a row that erupted into a volcano. Instead, he told of the time he had searched for a lost child and found the boy hiding behind boxes under his parents' bunk. Nina and Herbert laughed. Mary kept her head down and ate.

"You must see plenty of humorous things in your work in camp," Nina said, taking Jacob's empty plate. Her fingers brushed his, sending a tingle up his arm.

He started to tell her another story, just to hear her laugh, but Herbert began some of his own, regaling the women with tales of hasty marriages around camp. Jacob had noticed the same himself, but found no humor in it. In his experience, not that he had a lot, any long-term relationship should not be formed during times of intense danger or stress. He opened his mouth to state his opinion, but closed it at the starry-eyed look on Nina's face.

What was it about women that sent them into a dream state when marriage was mentioned?

"Are you performing all these marriages, Herbert?" Nina took his plate.

"Oh, no." He shook his head hard enough to loosen a well-oiled curl to flop across his forehead. "They are performed before I hear of them."

"A pastor who doesn't perform marriages?" Jacob accepted a mug of coffee from Nina. "That seems a bit strange."

Herbert's eyes widened. "Not really." The coffee he took from Nina seemed particularly interesting to the man.

Jacob caught Nina's narrow-eyed look. Good, she'd caught the man's trip of the tongue, also. He wondered how long it would take her to notice the man's sermons all sounded the same. Now suspicion grew at his statement. Did the man perform any marriages?

Mary also seemed to be curious at the man's words.

She glanced at him, then in the direction of the camp's entrance.

Perhaps Jacob needed to look through all the announcements posted on the bulletin board. There very well could be something Herbert would prefer Jacob and Nina not know. With the man spending so much time with Nina, Jacob needed to find out the truth.

"Would you care to take a walk with me, Nina?" Jacob set his cup next to her cooking fire and stood.

"Herbert?" Nina offered.

"Just you, please," Jacob said. "There is something I need to discuss with you. In private."

"Oh. Certainly."

"Mary and I can handle things here." Herbert's smile faded. "I'll see you when you return or at breakfast."

"That was rude," Nina said, as soon as they were out of hearing distance.

"My apologies." He pulled her into the shade of a tree. "There is something about Mr. Collins that rubs me wrong. Tell me you haven't noticed anything strange about him."

She took her lip between her teeth. "Possibly."

"I'm beginning to suspect he isn't really a man of God."

She crossed her arms. "Maybe he isn't ordained, but he can still have a heart hungry for the Word and have the desire to spread the Word. I think you're jumping to conclusions."

"I think you're too naive."

Her eyes sparked in the moonlight. "You need to learn to trust people. How can you go through life without opening your heart?"

His heart was open enough. He almost told her how open and how much she filled the hole he'd had for so long. "You are the most frustrating woman I've ever met."

"And you're the most infuriating man!" She stomped

her foot, looking so beautiful, that he chuckled. "Stop laughing at me. Oh!" She whirled and marched away.

He rushed to catch up to her. "I'm sorry."

"I hear the laughter in your voice."

"Let's walk on the beach."

She cut him a sideways glance. "Won't that be too romantic for your blood? What if you take ill?" She shook her head. "I think a romantic walk might be your undoing."

"I said I was sorry. Besides, it will be two friends walking off dinner. We've done it several times before."

She made a noise in her throat, but turned toward the sea. They walked through camp without speaking. Once they hit the beach, Nina plopped to the sand and, still not talking, removed her shoes.

"Are you going to remain silent the entire evening?" he asked.

"I might." She held out her hand for him to help her up.

He tugged her to her feet. "I'm sorry I criticized your friend."

She sighed. "That isn't why I'm angry."

"Then, why are you?"

"I can't tell you." Chin lifted high, she strolled to the water's edge, but not before he saw the glimmer of tears in her eyes.

His teasing had gone too far. He reached for her, pulling her close. "I'm so sorry," he whispered.

She raised shining eyes to his. Not able to help himself, he lowered his head, brushing his lips against hers. They were as soft as he'd imagined, like silk across the back of his hand. He deepened the kiss, sending his senses into overdrive.

The aroma of wet sand and sea mingled with the sweet scent of jasmine in her hair. The waves played with their toes and soaked the legs of Jacob's pants.

"I can't do this. You're leaving soon." She planted her fists on his chest and pushed.

She fell back into the surf, shrieking. Jacob lost his footing as he tried to grab her. He fell with a splash beside her.

She raised shocked eyes to his, then laughed, the melodious sound ringing across the beach. Scooping her hands, she splashed him.

"It's like that, is it?" He grabbed her hands, growing serious. "Come with me when I leave for Kansas." His request shocked him, but no more so than her, judging by the widening of her eyes.

She pulled free of his hold and staggered from the water. "I can't. I have responsibilities here." She turned and ran, grabbing her shoes from the sand and leaving him sitting in the water like a clump of seaweed.

Chapter 10

The next morning, camera in hand, Nina made her way to Nob Hill to photograph the destruction of San Francisco without the haze of fire and smoke overshadowing everything. While cleanup efforts were well underway, the city resembled a graveyard of once fine homes and businesses. She swallowed the lump in her throat and clicked the shutter button. It would be a good long while before the city was anywhere near its former splendor.

She sat on the grass, saddened by the destruction. Even after weeks had passed, the terror of the earthquake and destruction still hovered over the day-to-day happenings of the survivors.

Five dollars, payment for her last batch of photographs, crinkled in her pocket. A new roll of film poked her hip. Was it right of her to make money off the misfortune of others? She'd always thought of her pictures as letting the rest of the country know how San Francisco fared. Perhaps she was wrong. Perhaps it would have been best to take the pictures for free, but food wasn't cheap, and the children needed to eat.

Didn't God expect his children to be paid for their work? She'd always thought so. Man, or woman, could not live off ministry alone. Even a few funds were useful. Realizing her train of thought would get her nowhere, she transferred her thoughts to the night before and the feel of Jacob's kiss. A more dangerous path to dwell on for sure.

She ran her finger over her lips. Why had she pushed him away? What if she had said yes to his proposal of going to Kansas with him? No, she'd made the right choice. She couldn't leave the children alone, nor could she uproot them from all they had ever known. Especially little Abby, who still cried herself to sleep at night. They'd all lost so much already.

Pushing to her feet, Nina headed back to camp, stopping by the board where survivors left messages. At first, she had checked the boards every day, but had slacked off in the past few weeks. She ran her finger over the list of people looking for lost ones. There! Her heart leaped. Abby's parents were alive and living in the Presidio camp.

Oh, why hadn't they seen her note of finding Abby? She searched the stacks of papers. It must have fallen and blown away. No matter. The sun had brightened for one lost little girl.

Nina lifted her skirts and dashed to her tent. "Abby!" She scooped the child into her arms and spun. "Your mommy and daddy are looking for you. Come, sweetheart." Taking the little girl by the hand, she left the others in Mary's care, grateful the woman hadn't disappeared for the day yet.

Sending prayers of thanksgiving to heaven, and not wanting to wait another day, Nina led Abby through the littered streets to the other refugee camp. She searched the board there, looking for the location of the Hayfields. "There, sweetie. See? Your parents are in tent number one-twelve."

Excitement spurred Nina on. She had to force her steps to match the slower ones of the child. This was why she took in the children. Finding the family of even one lost child was worth the sacrifice of scanty meals and hours of drudging work.

A woman sat outside tent one-twelve, a toddler playing in the dirt at her feet. Abby cried out and let go of Nina's hand.

The woman glanced up, opened her arms and sobbed. "My baby."

Tears sprang to Nina's eyes at the reunion. She turned to go.

"Wait." The woman stood, keeping an arm around Abby. "Please. Have a cup of coffee with me. It's the least I can do."

Nina sniffed and nodded. "I've had her since a few days after the quake. A boy living with me found her."

"God bless you both." She held out a hand. "I'm Louellen."

"Nina." She took a seat on an overturned crate. "I'm sorry I didn't see your posting sooner."

"It is no matter. I have my little girl back." Louellen poured Nina a cup of watered-down coffee. "It isn't much, especially because of my gratitude."

Nina pulled the five dollars from her pocket. "Take this, please."

"No, it is my husband and I who owe you."

Nina put the money in the woman's hand and closed her fingers around her. "I want to. May I take your photograph? The eastern newspapers will like one of a happy reunion."

Louellen smiled and sat, gathering her children close to her. "My husband, Luke, will be so pleased. He has never stopped looking for our Abigail."

After taking their picture, Nina sipped at the coffee. "Abby said you were under the house."

"We were." Louellen shuddered. "Luke shoved Abby out of the way as the roof fell. By the grace of God, several beams kept the debris from crushing us. Still, it was almost two days before they found us, and Luke hasn't been able to do much because of cracked ribs." She rubbed her eyes with the hem of her stained apron. "He had shielded the baby and me with his body."

Nina remembered Jacob doing the same thing for her on the day of the quake. Oh, why was she so stubborn that she couldn't leave with him? Would it be so terrible for the children in her care to start a new life somewhere else? But, what if their parents were searching for them as Abby's had been? If she took the little ones away, they might never be reunited. Finding Abby's family had given her hope that the others would not be forever orphaned.

"Abby?" Nina turned to see a man, so thin his clothes hung on his frame, cry out as he rushed toward them.

She should go and leave the family to reunite in peace. She set down her cup and stood.

"No, Nina, stay." Louellen waved her down, then glanced at her husband. "This kind woman has brought our daughter back."

Mr. Hayfield clasped Nina's hands in his calloused ones. "Praise God for your kindness."

Uncomfortable under the man's grateful gaze, Nina pulled free. "I was happy to care for her. She is a doll."

"That's my girl." He grabbed Abby to his chest. "Please, miss, if there is anything I can ever do to repay you, let me know."

"I don't require payment." Nina grinned. "I really must go. I have others to watch out for. If you need me, I'm in the Golden Gate Park." Heart filled with gratitude and happiness, she bid them farewell and headed for home.

She passed butchers set up in the street, selling meat. She reached for her money, then remembered she had given it away. Still smiling, she waved.

"Here." The butcher waved her over. "I heard what you did for those people." He shoved paper-wrapped beef into her hands. "For your stew pot."

"Thank you." She hoped to share it with Jacob despite her embarrassment over falling into the ocean, then running away like a frightened rabbit.

She passed a fallen warehouse that had once held fine china. Scores of men combed through the wreckage. She doubted they would find anything useful, unless the building had been guarded against looters. Beautiful dishes were a thing of the past to be rarely seen again. Perhaps far in the future.

"The ferry is running again," someone shouted. "We can leave the city."

"It's been running for weeks," another man yelled. "What planet have you been living on?"

Nina laughed and continued on her way. How much would the camps empty once word spread that folks could leave? Or would the survivors stay because San Francisco was home? Nina wanted to see the city rebuilt, and do her part to restore things to their former splendor. She may not be able to build new homes, but she could help the people around her.

"Miss!" A young woman, skirts swishing around bony knees, sprinted toward her. "I heard you had found a child and had others. Do you perhaps have a little boy named Ethan?"

Nina grinned. "I do. A little towhead around the age of three. He was found wandering Market Street."

The woman sagged to the ground. "He is my son. My husband died in the quake, and I lost my boy during the commotion afterward."

Nina helped her to her feet. "Come with me."

Together, they made their way to Nina's tent where the

woman was reunited with her son. By now, tears flowed freely down Nina's face. Despite how her heart yearned to be with Jacob, she had confirmation that staying and helping was what she was meant to do.

"Where are you staying?" Nina asked.

"Wherever I can. I move around a lot, looking for Ethan."

"How would you like to stay with me?" Nina said. "I can always use the help." She refused to think of what Jacob would say when he heard she had taken in another.

Jacob folded his hands behind his back and stared at a poster tacked to the board. A marriage bureau? Find your lifelong mate for only two dollars? Was he really seeing what he thought he was seeing? Someone was charging people in order to find them a spouse. No wonder there were so many marriages in camp.

Who was responsible? He glanced around him. It wasn't against the law, per se, but it was a bit unethical. He eyed yet another person selling cheap wedding rings. So many people tried to find ways to make easy money off folks who had little to begin with. He glanced again at the poster, noted the tent number and started his afternoon patrol.

"Jacob." Nina hurried toward him. "I've got beef. Would you like to stop by for supper? I'm afraid it will be stew again, but at least there will be fresh meat."

"You aren't angry with me?"

"Of course not. I behaved like a silly schoolgirl."

He grinned. "Then may I kiss you again?"

She slapped his shoulder. "You may not."

"Pity." He winked, delighting at the blush that colored her cheeks. "They have built a few wooden temporary houses on the outskirts of camp." Jacob's heart leaped at the look of joy on her face. "I've put your name on the list to receive one."

"Oh, good. I found Abby's parents, and the mother of one of my little boys, but the mother and son will be living with me. I desperately need more room."

Jacob sighed. "You need a warehouse."

"Do you know of one?" Her eyes twinkled.

"None standing empty, with standing being the important thing." He placed his arm around her shoulder, the same as he would a male friend. What he wanted to do was take her hand like two people courting would do. He wouldn't, though, for fear it would cause her to run away again. "Let's cook this meat before it rots."

When they arrived, Jacob nodded at Herbert and studied the pretty young woman who snuggled with a toddler boy. This must be Nina's newest addition. Nothing about the woman dug up any warning signs. He eyed the meat in Nina's arms. It wouldn't stretch far.

"I've carrots and potatoes," Herbert said. "We'll have a substantial stew tonight, not that I'm complaining."

Jacob snorted. Sounded like ungratefulness to him. Where did the man get the hard-to-come-by items? Jacob studied his spotless suit and slicked-back hair, noticing for perhaps the first time, that the man, while living in a refugee camp, seemed to have it better than most. He also definitely seemed to have his cap set for Nina.

Jacob shrugged. Maybe she returned Herbert's affections and that was why she had rejected his kiss at the beach. An upstanding woman such as Nina would do that exact thing if she had an understanding with one man while another made advances. Shame flooded through him. This would be the last dinner invitation he accepted. Nina had made her choice. Who was Jacob, a man so torn and confused regarding his emotions, that he should interfere with Nina's chance at happiness?

Once he told her of his suspicions regarding Herbert,

he would step aside and let her come to her own conclusion. Despite the aroma of cooking beef, he had lost his appetite. He wouldn't stay. Instead, he would say what needed saying and leave. There would be more food to go around that way, and his heart wouldn't ache as Herbert courted Nina.

"There is a marriage bureau in town," he said, watching Herbert's face. "Someone is charging people to get married." He nodded his thanks as Nina handed him a cup of coffee, no doubt also provided by Herbert. "Now, that alone is not against the law, but if said person is not certified to perform these marriages, that is a different story."

Herbert said nothing, instead keeping his focus on the mug in his hand.

"You seem to be able to get your hands on quite a lot of goods, Herbert." Jacob kept a sharp eye on the man, noticing the high color on his cheeks.

"Herbert?" Nina stopped stirring the stew. "What is Jacob talking about?"

He set his mug on the ground. "I'm a shop owner, or maybe a former one, depending on how you look at it. I have a small storage building untouched by fire."

"You've been keeping the things for yourself?" Nina paled.

"No, I've been sharing with you and the children."

"Others could also benefit greatly from what you so sparingly give." She tucked a wayward strand of hair behind her ear, revealing a flushed cheek. "Are you responsible for these hasty weddings? Are you ordained?"

"I am not ordained." He hung his head.

"And?"

"I am charging two dollars to find someone a bride or groom, then performing the wedding."

"When we asked you before, you said you weren't performing them." Nina gasped, covering her mouth with her hand. "None of them are legal. You lied to me."

"I hope you kept records," Jacob said, standing. "I will be posting a notice alerting all the people you've swindled. Good evening, Nina, I will not be staying to eat." He headed to his own tent.

"Wait." Nina caught up with him. "Please stay. I'll send Herbert away. With your enlistment duty almost over, we have so little time left."

He gazed at her face, wanting very much to kiss her again. "I'm sorry if I ruined your courtship with Herbert." He twined a strand of blond silk around his finger.

"Don't be silly." Her husky response was almost his undoing. "We aren't courting. I enjoyed Herbert's attention as any girl would, but there can be nothing between us now. While I will forgive him, I can no longer trust him."

"What about between us?" He ran the back of his knuckles down her jaw.

"That is up to you." She closed her eyes.

"Hmm. Because of my views regarding God and responsibility." His spirits sank.

"Why can't you see that you are already more than you believe?" She opened her eyes, the longing there, stealing his breath. "You have cared very well for the refugees. And me."

He wanted to believe her, but every thought of caring for others dredged up the horror of his past. He exhaled sharply and stepped away. A bitter wind blew through his heart.

With pain clouding her eyes, Nina turned and walked away. She seemed to do that a lot because of him. He almost called her back, promising her everything she wanted and more. Instead, he headed for the shadows. A place that suited him.

After marching around the perimeter of the camp, he neared the common area and heard the sounds of scuffling. He burst into the clearing. Two men punched and kicked at a third who curled into a ball on the ground.

"Hey, there!" Jacob rushed forward, realizing then that Herbert was the one being beaten. "What is going on here?"

"This man has caused me to commit fornication," one said, waving a hand-printed poster in the air advertising marriages. "Rumor around camp is that he ain't a real preacher."

The other nodded. "It turns out we aren't married to our wives as we thought."

"Clear out," Jacob said, holding out a hand to Herbert. "I'll take care of this."

The men left. Jacob handed Herbert his handkerchief so he could wipe his bloody lip. "I admire a man who can admit his transgressions. Looks like you're spreading the word on your own. You did post the new fliers, correct?"

"For what it's worth." Herbert dabbed his lip and tried to return Jacob's handkerchief.

"Keep it. I'll walk you home to prevent any more of this violence."

"I'll make an announcement at Sunday service. I guess my days of preaching are finished."

"I reckon so." Jacob escorted him home.

"You're a good man, Sergeant." Herbert put a hand on the flap tent. "May I ask you a personal question?"

"You may. It doesn't mean I will answer."

"Fair enough." Herbert took a deep breath. "Why have you not asked for Nina's hand? Any fool can see how you feel about each other."

"We desire different things in life."

Herbert clapped him on the shoulder. "You need to figure out what is more important, my friend. A woman like Nina will not last long."

Jacob agreed. He did need to spend a lot of time searching his heart. "Good evening."

Him a good man? He wasn't sure. What if he had exposed Herbert, not only for the good of those he had falsely performed ceremonies for, but so the other man could not court Nina until Jacob figured out what it was he wanted?

He fell asleep that night feeling lower than he had ever felt before.

Chapter 11

Nina sat on the recovering ground of Nob Hill, her legs bent, chin resting on her knees, and her camera sitting unused beside her. She focused on a building she thought might have once been a bank. Maybe a large house. She wasn't familiar with this side of the city. Still, the cleanup process, no matter how small, gave her hope.

Five men worked, tossing bricks into the back of a wagon. She imagined she could see the sweat on their brows, the perspiration staining their shirts. Men who possibly had little to eat yet gave up their days to help the city rebuild. God would bless their efforts, she was certain.

While she watched, she mulled over Herbert's deception. True, no one could fault the man for trying to make a living in those difficult times. What bothered her was the lies. Why pretend to be a pastor? He may not have forced couples to wed, but he had definitely misled them, not having the proper credentials to perform the marriages. She'd skipped breakfast, escaping to the hill, rather than take the chance he might stop by as usual.

While her heart tended to yearn for Jacob, her mind had told her she needed to focus potential marriage prospects in Herbert's direction. Or it had, until the day before. She sighed. Jacob would be leaving, his heart still not right with God, and Herbert was a liar. Were there no good unmarried men left in San Francisco?

"Good morning."

She turned and shaded her eyes to see Jacob smiling down at her. Her heart leaped. Had he sought her out or happened upon her unaware? She hoped it was the first option.

He sat beside her. "What are you doing?"

"I've decided to come here every morning at the same time to watch the progress being made on that building." She pointed to where she'd been looking. "It gives me hope to see the progress."

"Are you losing hope?" The concerned look on his face almost made her cry.

She shook her head and looked away. "Not too much."

"I believe that building was once the Mark Hopkins Institute."

She gasped. "Please tell me they saved some of the artwork."

"Most of it. The fire gave warning of its approach. A shame about the beautiful building, though."

She nodded, thinking of all the other grand places that had succumbed to the fire, if not the earthquake. "The cleanup crew and builders are making great progress, but I'm sure you aren't here to reminisce with me."

"I came to tell you that your cottage is ready."

She blinked. "It is? You must have pulled some strings, Jacob, but aren't there others in more need than me?"

"You and the children need a better place to live. The rent is two dollars a month. Can you afford that?"

"Of course. Between the income from my photographs and Johnny's rats, we will manage just fine." She didn't need to tell him that photos of the type she had once taken were becoming fewer. She would need to find other human interest stories to photograph.

"I have a few hours if you need help transferring your belongings," Jacob said.

"That is greatly appreciated. Thank you." She held out her hand for him to help her up.

"I also heard you were no longer accepting free food."

She shook her head. "Others need it more, and I do have a few dollars. Small stores are popping up here and there. I'm sure even Herbert is back into the shop business, now that his secret is out."

"You also care for six other people besides yourself. You must be sleeping on top of each other."

She laughed. "In a sense. We've managed to stack the cots and put mattresses on the ground under them. By spending most of our time outside, we get along well. The cottage will enable us to put up shelves, giving us even more floor space."

Excitement welled in her. Her "family" would have a roof over their heads, something other than canvas stiffened by the salty sea air.

"I'll show you your new home before I help you move. You can plan in your head where you want to put things."

He led her away from the Golden Gate Park to the Presidio. She hadn't been aware that she might have to move that far and was even more grateful for his offer of help.

Beside the ten-by-fourteen-foot cottage sat a can of paint. Nina glanced at Jacob.

"I'd hoped to have it painted before I showed it to you. It's turquoise. That's all I could find."

She clapped her hands. "It will be beautiful. I can have Johnny paint it easily enough. Thank you." Despite his resolve to leave her when he moved back to Kansas, he did care. She saw it in his kind gift and the soft look in his eyes. Instead of making her happy, the knowledge increased her sadness. She almost wished he would move and get it over with. If he were gone, her heart could begin healing.

She opened the door to the cottage, glad to see how well the two windows lit up the space. If she placed a stove in the corner, a small table beside it, shelves along the wall, they could build bunks for them all to sleep on. It would still be tight, but more room than they had now. It was almost a mansion compared to the tent. "I need a stove."

"That has been arranged and should arrive by tomorrow."

"How much?"

"It's taken care of."

"How much?" She put her hands on her hips.

He sighed. "Two dollars."

She dug the money from her pocket and held it out. "Please, take it. I want to be self-sufficient. While I appreciate all you do for me, you'll be leaving. I need to grow used to relying on myself."

"What if I decide to stay?" His eyes darkened.

"What if you do?" She squared her shoulders. "Will that change anything between us?"

"I'd like to think so."

"Have you changed your views on my taking in orphans and on God's presence in all this?"

"I'm working on it."

"Come see me when you've completed working on it." She stormed out the door. If not for those in her care, she'd be tempted to refuse the cottage. Tears trickled down her cheeks as she marched in the direction of the park.

It wouldn't take long to pack up. She could rent a wagon easily enough. Everyone was happy to earn a few dollars. With Mary and little Ethan's mother, Agnes, they would manage.

"Nina, wait." Jacob spun her to face him. "I'm sorry. Whatever I said to upset you, I'm sorry."

"The fact you don't know what you said upsets me further." Had he learned nothing in the time they've known each other? Had she had no effect on him? She pulled free of his grasp before he could see that sobs threatened, clogging her throat.

He sighed and matched his steps with hers. "I will help you move, then head back to my own tent."

So, he wouldn't be moving to the Presidio compound. She wouldn't see him every day. It was for the best. But, that didn't make the pain any easier to bear.

As they approached her tent, she forced a smile to her lips. "Gather our things, ladies," she said to Mary and Agnes. "We're moving to a real house."

Mary's eyes widened. Agnes leaped to her feet with a shout of joy and rushed into the tent, calling Ethan's name.

"Are you serious, Miss Hansen?" Johnny held his empty burlap bag.

"Very serious, Mr. Smith." She patted his shoulder. "If you can put aside your rat hunting for a day or two, I've some jobs for you to do."

"Yes, ma'am!"

Several minutes later, a wagon stopped in front of the tent. Nina met Jacob's gaze. He shrugged. "I hired it yesterday."

The man was hopeless, but oh, how she would miss him.

Their few things barely filled the wagon halfway. Nina climbed next to the driver while the others piled into the back. As they pulled away from their former home, she glanced back to see Jacob watching them drive away.

She sniffed and wiped her eyes on the sleeve of her blouse. It was for the best. If only she could convince her heart.

Shame and confusion clouded his mind. All Jacob wanted was to ease Nina's burden. Why couldn't she understand?

He set off to follow the wagon, hoping he would arrive in time to help unload. If not, he would find wood to stack against the house for her stove. She might resent his help, but being a smart woman, wouldn't refuse it, not really. She'd fuss and shove money at him, but for the sake of the children, would accept what he offered.

He could suggest the other women stay in the tent she had vacated, but knew Nina would convince them to stay with her in the cottage. Once she set her mind on helping someone, there was no stopping her. He smiled. It was one of the things he loved about her.

Loved? Yes, he did love her, and that alone kept him pondering his future deep into the night as he lay on his hard cot. She felt the same for him, he felt it deep inside. Still, with his future undecided, he needed to keep the words to himself.

He stopped in front of a building that resembled an outhouse more than anything else, but was in fact, a bakery. He purchased six meat pastries before continuing on his way to the Presidio. He passed a house, once home to an influential family. A sign in the window stated it was for sale. Nina would love the old place. It had plenty of rooms she could fill with homeless children. Unfortunately, he also knew the impossibility of her being able to afford such a home.

The wagon was just pulling away from the cottage when Jacob arrived. "I've brought dinner," he said, holding out the bag to Nina.

She exhaled sharply. "Stop helping me."

"You've fed me plenty of times." After taking out one of the pastries, he handed her the bag. "I thought you might be tired after the move, and I can help build the bunks."

"Is that where the boards came from?" She pointed to a stack salvaged from collapsed buildings.

"Yes. I'm glad they got here so soon. I thought it would please you to build with wood taken from damaged buildings."

"It does, thank you." She gave him a ghost of a smile and handed out the pastries.

The smiles on the children's faces made the cost of the dinner worth it in Jacob's estimation.

The woman, Mary, avoided his gaze, as usual, and ducked into the house with her dinner. There was something fishy about her manner, but since Nina didn't seem to have any complaints, it was none of Jacob's business. His suspicions about Herbert, even though born through jealousy, had proven true.

After eating, he grabbed the hammer and box of nails next to the wood and headed inside to measure for the bunk beds. Mary was rummaging through a box he assumed belonged to Nina, judging from the blouse sticking out. He'd seen her wear it on many occasions. When he entered, Mary closed the box and stepped back, scuttling past him to go outside. He shook his head. Strange woman, that one. She would definitely bear watching.

Lacking a tape measure, he used his hands and fingers to judge the space. Not the most accurate way of measuring, but it worked in a pinch. He would have the beds built and mattresses on before bedtime.

"Why didn't you work today?" Nina leaned against the door frame.

"I asked for it off in order to help you. I'll still have time to make my rounds before going to sleep." It wasn't difficult to get the time away with only weeks of his enlistment left. "I may stay on for a while before heading to Kansas," he said. "I can join in with the reconstruction."

She said nothing, only gave him a nod, before stepping to the other side of the room. "Johnny!"

"Yes, ma'am." The young man hurried to her side.

"I need shelves here and here." She pointed to places on the wall. "Then, if you can manage, a table about this size—" she held her arms wide "—to go here. We'll sit on crates until I find chairs."

"I can build those things for you." Jacob shoved the hammer into his waistband.

"Johnny has trained as a carpenter at the orphanage. He can build a simple project such as this."

He shook his head and headed back to the stack of wood. Her frigid but polite manner chipped at his heart. He needed to act the same. Distance between them would make his leaving easier. And he needed to leave. Even if he decided to stay in San Francisco, he would need to do something with his family land. After all, the farm was being looked after by a family friend. It would be in good condition should he decide to return.

The chatter of the two little boys competed with the grating of the saw. Their laughter as they and the puppy chased a ball, warmed him. He could see a bit of why children meant so much to Nina. Well, that and the fact she had grown up as an orphan. Still, the responsibility was a heavy burden for just one person.

He chuckled, realizing that despite his earlier resolve not to get involved, he now spent his day off building furniture for Nina's very own home for the lost. Perhaps she had found something he had lost years ago when the fire had taken his family. Was it possible for him to regain what was lost?

Nina and Agnes chattered like a couple of seagulls as they sorted through cans of food. The sounds of a home wrapped Jacob as effectively as a blanket dried by the sun. He had missed the sound of family. More than he cared to admit. Unfortunately, the family in front of him wasn't his.

The sun had set by the time the last bunk was placed against the wall. There was now room for six people to sleep, the amount of people now living in the cottage, plus one more. Jacob knew that if Nina had her way, there would soon be young ones sleeping on the floor or sharing bunks, as well.

"I'm finished." He squatted next to where she doused the fire, which she had built in front of the cottage. "Care to take a walk with me?"

She shook her head. "Is that wise? Wouldn't it be better for us to part ways now?"

He straightened. "What do you mean?"

"With me living here and you there, you can go about your business and leave me to mine." She stood, her gaze caressing his face. "Oh, Jacob. We want different things from life. Kansas sounds wonderful, but I am needed here. I don't have the luxury to think of myself."

She thought him selfish. Even now, despite all that he had done for the refugees and the city, she thought he did it out of duty, or because it was his job, not because he wanted to.

"Very well." He marched away, not looking back, even when he heard her sob.

Maybe he had started out helping from a sense of duty, but that had vanished long ago when he'd met a selfless, kindhearted woman named Nina Hansen. She could send him away, but she couldn't make him stay away. He would still keep an eye on her during his remaining days, helping where he saw a need.

Once inside his tent, he unclothed, not bothering to drape his uniform over a chair as was his habit. Nina's rejection had cut deep. Instead, visions of her on the beach, the waves rolling over her feet, filled his mind. The thought of her, alone and sad on top of Nob Hill, watching the slow progression of rebuilding a city, consumed his thoughts.

He wanted to head back to her cottage in the morning and paint for her, but doubted his efforts would be welcomed.

"Sir!"

Jacob sat upright, grabbing for his pants. Shoving his legs into them, he commanded the soldier outside to enter.

"Sir." The private saluted. "We've several people outside with complaints of thievery."

"Come again?" Jacob shook his head to clear it of thoughts of Nina.

"There has been a rash of thefts in camp over the last week. Witnesses state the culprit looks like one of the women living with your woman friend."

"At ease, soldier." Jacob grabbed his shirt. "I'll be out in a moment."

Thefts? He'd thought Mary up to no good. Somehow, he didn't think the thief could be Agnes. She wouldn't take the chance of leaving her son behind if she were arrested.

Back in uniform, he stepped outside to face the crowd. Tomorrow, he would visit Nina on official business. She would be less happy to see him than ever.

Chapter 12

A rap on the door pulled Nina away from breakfast preparations. She glanced at Agnes, who shrugged. Mary had left before Nina had gotten up, but she wouldn't knock, would she? Unless her arms were full of purchases. The woman did seem to bring a lot of things into the house, despite no signs of a job. Since her purchases often supplied food or clothing for the children, Nina couldn't complain.

She opened the door to Herbert, who, wearing a new suit, stood with a sheepish grin on his face and flowers in his hand. She stepped out, pulling the door closed behind her. "What do you want?"

"These are for you." He thrust the flowers at her. "I've come to apologize."

"Have you now?" She narrowed her eyes, taking the flowers from his hand and laying them on the stoop. She wasn't one to be swayed by a suit and flowers.

"May we sit?" He motioned to a couple of stumps Johnny had dragged in front of the cottage the night before.

Nina nodded, still wary, and took her seat, arranging her skirts primly around her ankles in an effort not to meet his earnest gaze. He must know of her disappointment. Surely, he didn't expect a hearty welcome. The man had lied to her!

For several seconds, Herbert said nothing, simply stared

at the ground between his feet. Finally, he clapped his hands on his knees and met her gaze. "I don't know what to say, except I'm sorry."

"I thought you were a man of God."

"I am a man of faith. I only stumbled in the face of adversity and deeply regret having done so."

He looked so contrite, Nina couldn't help but put a hand on his arm. "You must make this right."

"I have been going tent to tent and have the marks to prove it."

She had noticed the faint bruises on his cheekbones and under one eye. She knew she should feel sorry for the abuse, but honestly couldn't bring herself to do so. Not that she was happy, but what he had done had repercussions. She hoped he could learn from them. All she could say was, "I forgive you. Come to breakfast."

"Thank you, but I must decline. I will come for dinner, if I may. There are still a lot of wronged people I need to see."

"I admire you for making amends."

He shrugged. "It is a small price to pay for my deception." He glanced around the outside of the small cottage. "I had expected to see the sergeant here."

"Our lives have parted ways." Saying the words woke the ever present pain in her heart. "He will be heading to Kansas soon."

His smile broadened. "Dare I hope we may be more than friends?"

"I'm afraid not." She smiled, hoping to soften the blow. "I'm resigned to being a spinster in care of orphans. I feel called to do so. I'm not sure there is room for a husband in my future."

"I have come to care about the children. May I still help where I can?"

"I won't turn down anything that benefits my charges." She held out her hand. "I'll see you at dinner."

Instead of a handshake, he lifted her hand to his lips, brushing them softly across her knuckles. "You are a remarkable woman, Nina Hansen. Until dinner." He dropped her hand and strolled away.

She wasn't sorry she had turned down his offer of something more than friendship. Her heart would, most likely, always belong to another. Taking a deep breath through her nose, she reentered the cottage and returned to breakfast preparations.

Agnes had finished the cooking and settled the three boys around the table. "I've fixed you a plate. Mary came across eggs yesterday. I have no idea how she does it."

Neither did Nina. Another knock sounded at the door before she could take her seat. Goodness, the cottage was busy that morning.

A woman in dirty and tattered clothing stood outside, her arms around an equally dirty child. "I heard you take in strays."

"Well, I—"

"I found this child weeks ago. I can't keep her no more. I have enough trouble feeding my own three." She thrust the toddler at Nina. "You take her. Said her name is Sally." The woman turned and shuffled away.

Nina stared after her, openmouthed, until the child started to cry. "Well," Nina said. "Welcome." She carried the little girl into the house and placed her in her own chair. "Everyone, this is Sally. She will be living with us now."

The three boys stared at the girl, then each other, then turned their attention back to their breakfast. Nina smiled. They did have their priorities, after all.

"How old are you, Sally? Do you know?" Nina asked.

"Tree." The child scooped eggs into her mouth with filthy hands.

Nina cringed. She should have washed her first, but the hunger on the child's face had made her wait. "Do you know your last name?"

"Sally."

Agnes chuckled. "I guess you can check the boards for anyone missing Sally Sally."

Nina grabbed a slice of bread—Sally having eaten her breakfast—and spread a thin layer of jam across the top. As she ate, she pondered the latest child, no doubt sporting lice in her tangle of red hair. "Was the woman who dropped you off your mommy?"

"No." Sally continued to eat. "Mommy fell in a hole."

The toast stuck in Nina's throat. Oh, the horrors the poor child must have seen. Tears stung her eyes. She doubted she would find anyone looking for a lost Sally, but she had to try.

Agnes met her gaze. "I'll clean her up. Go see what you can find out."

"Thank you." Nina patted Sally's head before rushing out the door. She really needed to find a place large enough to house her growing family. While grateful she had a solid roof over her head when so many didn't, they needed more space. With money so scarce, though, that was nothing more than a dream.

She passed a vendor selling meat pastries, the aroma reminding her of the last meal she had shared with Jacob. She glanced toward the ocean. Did he still take his daily strolls there? Did he miss having her by his side?

"Hello, lovely lady." A disheveled man reached for her arm.

Nina swiftly stepped out of his reach. Was it no longer wise to step outside alone? She glared at the man and continued to the camp's entrance. Shouts and cursing came from inside a nearby tent. Gambling, no doubt. She curled her lip, hoping Johnny wouldn't be enticed by such nonsense. Those lewd pursuits could ruin his ambitions toward finding an apprenticeship someday.

Soldiers marched in two straight lines toward the tent, two of them disappearing inside. The shouts grew louder and men dashed outside, scattering in all directions. Nina leaped out of the way in order not to be trampled, and snapped a photograph. She had seen more soldiers on patrol than ever before. Was the Golden Gate Park having the same problems with illegal activities? She prayed for Jacob's safety, hoping his commanding officer had sent sufficient help if troubles were escalating.

She finally arrived at the lost-and-found board. No one searched for a child by the name of Sally. Her heart fell. Another orphan of the earthquake.

A notice caught her attention. She pulled the newspaper clipping free and read how families in the east were looking to adopt orphans from the San Francisco area. Maybe one of them would take Sally. Nina couldn't bear to part with Johnny and little Sam, but other children might be able to find homes in other states. She made note of the contact information, added Sally's name to the board and then headed home.

Once there, she snapped a picture of the now clean and angelic Sally. Nina would put the photograph in the next day's mail and pray for a good family to come for the child. Perhaps she could post a notice in the camp saying she would do the same for other orphans, thus relieving the burdens of those who had no intentions of keeping the children. Maybe Jacob would help her interview prospective parents. The children couldn't leave with just anyone.

Nina needed to know they would be safe, well cared for and loved.

If she could find them families elsewhere, maybe someday, when the city was rebuilt, she could consider moving to another state. But not before. More children would come to her as a result of the quake. She needed to be here.

Mary barged through the door, almost knocking Nina over in the process and dropped a heavy bag on one of the lower bunks. She pulled the blanket over the bag, making it look like a pillow, then poured herself a cup of coffee.

"Where do you go each day?" Nina asked. "Have you found employment?"

"Of a sorts." The woman carried her coffee outside.

Nina followed. "What sort? The assortment of things you bring home are quite varied."

"Why all the questions? My contributions benefit everyone." Mary scowled.

"True, but…" Nina didn't want to mention how furtive the woman looked each time she arrived home, but her actions were very suspicious. "I'm only curious. Does your employer have room for others who want to make an honest living?"

Mary snorted. "Don't know about that. My employer is a greedy man. And a dangerous one. It's best you steer clear of him."

Mary. Out in the open like an honest woman and speaking with Nina. His heart leaped at the sight of Nina's golden head bent low to speak to the other woman.

Jacob stepped on a twig. The snap alerted the women, Mary taking off like a shot into the house.

Nina's face flushed as she straightened. She folded her hands in front of her. "Jacob, would you like a cup of coffee?"

"I'm here on official business this time."

"Oh?" Her brow wrinkled.

"The woman, Mary, has been accused of theft."

She paled, but didn't look surprised.

"Were you aware of this?"

"I've only just now suspected." She glanced over her shoulder. "What will you do?"

"I need to question her before determining that." He hated how formal he sounded.

"I'll bring her outside. I don't want the children to hear." She stepped inside, returning moments later with a sullen-faced Mary.

"I've done nothing." The woman glared.

"You were seen, just this morning, fleeing camp with a bag. Fetch it, please." Jacob stood military erect, his gaze as sharp as he could make it.

"If you want it, go and get it."

"Very well." He stepped inside the cottage. Several childish faces stared at him, along with the woman Agnes. "Where is the bag Mary brought in this morning?"

Johnny pointed to one of the bunks.

Jacob flipped back the army issue blanket. He dumped out the bag, seeing a gold bracelet, several articles of clothing and a wallet. He shoved everything back into the bag and marched outside.

Nina stood in front of Mary, legs spread and arms crossed. "She tried to flee."

"Thank you for detaining her." He shook the bag at Mary. "Here are the most recent stolen items. Where are the others?"

"I don't have them."

"Where are they?"

"My boss has them."

"A name, please."

"He'll kill me if I tell you."

"You'll be in jail. He can't harm you there."

"Jacob!" Nina lifted her chin. "Don't be so harsh. Can't you tell she's frightened?"

"She's a crook. She should be afraid of the law." Nina's naivety would get her in serious trouble someday. He bent over Mary. "A name!"

She shrank back. "Ira Barton. He lives on the outskirts of the Golden Gate Park. I ain't the only one working for him, either."

"Oh, Mary, how could you?" Nina plopped onto a stump. "We've been eating and wearing what belonged to others. You've involved us all."

"Let's go." Jacob reached for Mary.

"No, Jacob," Nina cried. "Mary, tell him you won't steal again."

He sighed. "Don't be foolish. If she doesn't go to jail, she'll be forced to steal. This is for her protection. Can't you see that?"

"There must be another way." Nina stood and moved between him and Mary. "She won't survive in prison. Look at her. She doesn't weigh more than a child."

"It's out of my hands."

"She could help you."

"No."

"Then I will leave here." She crossed her arms. "The others and I will leave the city, taking Mary with us."

She wouldn't. He studied her determined face. She would. "What do you suggest?"

"I know she didn't want to steal, did you, Mary?"

She shook her head. "He made me. Mr. Barton found me after the quake and promised me an easy life. He fed me and clothed me. I believed him. After a few days, I was told to steal and give him half of what I found or he would

cast me out. I had nowhere to go. You must believe me."
Tears streaked her face. "He has my daughter."

Despite the woman's crimes, Jacob was torn by her
story and by the stricken look on Nina's face. How could
he disappoint her again?

"I will help you if you will get my daughter back." Mary
clasped her hands in front of her.

Against his better judgment, Jacob nodded. "If you steal
again, I will have no other choice than to arrest you."

"Thank you." Nina smiled, the sight lifting Jacob's spirits. Maybe he had taken his first step toward repairing
their friendship.

He nodded. "I'll have that coffee now, if you don't
mind." He followed the women into the house, taking note
that a charming red-haired girl had been added to the mix.
He sat at the table where the little minx climbed promptly
onto his lap. He breathed deep of her freshly washed hair
and felt the tension ease from his shoulders. He barely took
notice that Nina snapped his picture.

Without removing the child from his lap, he accepted
the mug of coffee, its aroma mingling with scents of bak-
ing bread and the rose water used to wash the child's hair.
A picture of Nina standing in front of a stove in a larger
house, children playing on the floor, their smiles greeting
him when he returned home from a hard day's work rose
in his mind. Loneliness assailed him. At that moment, he
made his decision as to which path to take when his enlistment was done. But, before he could say so to Nina,
there was something else he needed to do. Something that
would heal them both. Until then, he still had a job to do.

"Johnny, a question, please." Jacob sipped his coffee.
"In your work, have you perhaps heard of a man by the
name of Ira Barton?"

The young man glanced at Nina, who nodded for him

to answer. "Yes, sir. He's not the type you want to get too close to. Meaner than a shark, that one. He has tried to take my rat money a time or two."

Jacob's grip tightened on the handle of his mug. He had no use for a man who preyed on women and children. He vowed that the last thing he would do as an enlisted man was to arrest Ira Barton.

After he finished his coffee, he reluctantly set the little girl on the floor, then motioned his head for Nina to step outside with him. "I miss you." He hadn't meant to blurt out the words. They exploded from his mouth as if they had a mind of their own.

She blinked back tears. "Nothing has changed, has it?"

He knew he had said it before, but he still said, "I'm working on it."

"I can see that, especially with your kindness to Mary."

"I expect her to help me. It will be very dangerous."

"I know, but she has a chance now."

Nina was right. If Mary was telling the truth, a crook would be behind bars soon and no longer able to force innocent people to do his bidding. "I don't want you to come, tomorrow, I mean, when I send Mary to Barton's tent."

"You have a plan?"

"Yes." He hoped it was a good one, but it would be dangerous, and the danger could come knocking on Nina's door. Jacob needed to make sure that didn't happen. "Will you walk with me? There is something I want to discuss with you."

She gave him a wary look, but nodded. His heart lurched to know he was the cause of the discomfort between them. "It's about Mary's dilemma."

She seemed to relax a bit and stepped beside him. Although she refused the crook of his arm, she allowed him to lead the way to the ocean, hoping the view would relax her further.

Instead, she sighed upon first glance at the waves and cast him a frustrated look as if he were the densest person she had ever met. Maybe he was. Clearly, he was missing something important.

Without taking off her shoes, she sat in the sand. "Tell me about your plan."

"This is usually out of my jurisdiction," he said, sitting beside her, "but if I were to go to the police, Mary would be behind bars within the hour. Instead, I will give her items each day that she can say she stole as she goes to Barton, and I will follow her."

"A sound plan, but I think there is something you are leaving out."

He touched her arm. "It's quite possible Barton will discover my plan. I'm sure he knows where Mary is staying. You could be in danger."

She rested her chin on her bent knees. "Then I will be on my guard."

"What about the children? Aren't you concerned for their safety?"

"Of course, I am." She glared. "But, this is our home. I'm not going anywhere."

He had feared that would be her answer.

Chapter 13

Nina waited a few minutes after Jacob left with Mary, then grabbed her camera and followed. She knew the way and was certain she would catch up to them by the time they reached Barton's tent.

She shoved aside her pain and confusion from the night before. Why had Jacob taken her to the beach? Did he not know what it had come to mean to her? That was *their* place. The place where he had kissed her and sent her heart spiraling. Instead of telling her what she so desired to hear, that he was staying in the city and had made his peace with God, he had kept the conversation focused on the business at hand. The man was hopeless. Still, the look on his face as he had held little Sally promised that change was happening in his heart.

Now was not the time to dwell on such things. Nina ducked behind a tree as Jacob darted into his tent, returning a few moments later with a box. It was a dangerous game the man played, giving away his possessions to catch an evil man. Why couldn't Jacob see what everyone around him knew? Did he think so little of himself he couldn't see that he was a good man? A man willing to keep safe the people in his charge?

Jacob handed Mary the box, then waited while she weaved through the spaces between tents. He glanced

Nina's way. She gasped and froze behind the tree's cover. When she peered around the trunk again, he was gone.

Which way? Mary had said Barton resided on the out-skirts of the camp, but had not given a tent number. That could be one of four directions. Nina groaned. She should have been upfront about wanting to accompany them. Jacob would have said no, but perhaps she could have convinced him.

A hand tapped her on the shoulder. She whirled and screamed, coming face-to-face with a disgruntled Jacob.

"What are you doing here?" His eyes flashed.

"Oh, I, uh…was going for a walk?"

"Are you asking me or telling me?" He crossed his arms, drawing attention to the muscles straining his shirt. "You were following Mary and me. Don't deny it."

"Fine. I was." Mercy, she didn't think his face could get any redder.

"Go home, Nina."

"You no longer have any jurisdiction over me." She squared her shoulders. "I have as much right to be here as you do. Remember, you're doing this without the ap-proval of your supervisor. What would your command-ing officer say?"

His mouth dropped open. "Are you threatening me?"

"No, I just really want to come."

"Why?"

"What if something happens to Mary, or to you? You'll need someone to go for help."

"You're grasping at air. Go home." He turned and marched away.

She lifted her camera. If she followed, she might pos-sibly catch a likeness of Barton, thus making it easier for the authorities to identify him. Otherwise, Jacob would have to catch the man firsthand, and that could cause trouble for everyone. What if Barton used violence against Jacob? The thought of him leaving tore at her heart. But if he died? It would feel like her heart had been ripped out of her chest. No, she needed to follow, staying out of the way, of course, and take her pictures which could possibly be used in some lawful way.

She had a purpose. Jacob needed to listen to reason. Keeping her distance, she continued to follow him, ducking behind tents when he turned. Far ahead, Mary rushed from between two tents, the box clutched to her chest.

When she stopped in front of a tent, the entrance blocked by a large man, Nina hid behind a tree. Jacob did the same a few yards ahead. Nina clicked the shutter on her camera as fast as she could, which wasn't nearly fast enough. He disappeared before she could capture his image.

Mary entered the tent. Nina moved along the narrow pathway behind the row of temporary canvas homes until she came within earshot.

Jacob grabbed her arm. "Why won't you listen to me?" he hissed. "Don't you understand I'm looking out for your well-being?"

"I'm doing the same for you." She pulled free. "You'll thank me someday."

"I doubt it." He pulled her into a crouch.

"It's all I've got, sir." Mary's voice quavered through the canvas wall. "With people coming and going and reconstruction taking so long, folks don't have much."

"The boss told you that if you don't bring in enough income, you'll have to start earning your keep on your back."

Jacob put a hand over Nina's mouth to stifle her gasp. "Barton isn't here. Let's go." He pulled her a few tents away.

"But, Mary."

"She'll come as soon as she's able. I need to tell my commanding officer what's going on."

Fear for her friend threatened to choke her. Spots swam before her eyes. Somehow, she needed to find a way to help her friend before the man could make good on his threat. This time when Jacob told her to go home, she followed his advice and headed toward the camp's entrance.

Before she reached it, a groan drew her into a stand of trees. "Hello?"

The groan came louder, spurring Nina to action. She slapped branches away from her face, falling to her knees beside Herbert. His left eye was swollen shut. Bruises covered his face and he clutched his side. "Oh, Herbert." Nina glanced around. She needed to get him to her cottage, but how?

She stepped back into the sunshine, looking, hoping, that Jacob was still in sight. He wasn't. "Hold on, Herbert, I'm going for help." She hitched her skirts and ran for Jacob's tent, hoping he hadn't left yet.

"Hold on there, missy." The man she had seen standing outside Barton's tent stepped in her path. "You been taking pictures?"

"Not lately." She moved to step around him.

"I don't believe you. Give me the camera." He reached for it.

"I will not!" She jumped back. "This is my livelihood."

"I said, give it to me." He lunged forward. Jacob leaped from behind his tent and grabbed the man's shirt.

The sound of ripping fabric mingled with the man's cursing. He turned and swung, his fist connecting with Jacob's jaw, snapping his head back. Jacob stayed on his feet and threw a punch of his own before reaching for the pistol at his waist.

"Stand down, sir. I will use this. What is your business with the lady?"

"Just making conversation." The man wiped his hand across his bleeding lip. "She ought not to take people's pictures without their say-so."

"I doubt she's done that. Move on."

The man cursed again, tossed a glare at Nina, letting her know the matter wasn't settled, then left.

"Are you trying to send me to an early grave?" Jacob pulled a handkerchief from his pocket and wiped at a cut on his chin. "Because it's working."

"I am so glad to see you." She grabbed his arm and tugged him into the trees. "Herbert is wounded, and too heavy for me to help back to my cottage. Say you'll help us."

"Of course, I will. All you need to do is ask."

The warm look in his eyes almost brought tears to her own. What was God doing, letting a man such as Jacob steal her heart and muddle her mind?

He caressed her cheek. "Let me find a wagon so we can tend to your friend."

She nodded, leaning into his touch, then went to kneel next to Herbert. Jacob hurried away.

"Ah," Herbert said. "I've been foolish."

"How so?" She smoothed the hair off his sweaty brow.

"I had hoped there was still a chance for me to steal your heart, but I see there isn't. Your heart belongs to another. Your sergeant is a good man."

She sighed. "He is, but unfortunately, he isn't mine."

"I would argue the fact, but every breath is a sharp ache in my side."

"Rest. I will take care of you."

"What if the big brute comes back?"

"Then, Jacob will deal with him."

* * *

It wasn't too difficult to find a wagon willing to transport Herbert for the price of a few cans of food. Jacob led the driver to the spot where he had left Nina, then crashed through the trees. The sight of her gaze tenderly on Herbert's battered face was almost his undoing. Did she care for him? She couldn't. The man was a shyster. She was concerned because he was her friend, no more. Still, Jacob yearned for her to look at him that way.

He thrust his shoulder under Herbert's arm and helped him to the wagon bed. Once he was lying in the back, Nina by his side, Jacob climbed next to the driver and gave instructions on where to go. "I have a doctor meeting us," he said over his shoulder. "I'm sure the man will be waiting for us when we arrive."

"Thank you." Nina smiled. "You've thought of everything."

He had yet to speak with his commanding officer, but that could wait another hour or so. They passed Mary halfway between the two camps and stopped long enough for her to join Nina and Herbert in the back of the wagon. The woman remained silent, her shoulders slumped.

The morning hadn't gone exactly as Jacob had planned, but he would find a way for the woman to escape her life and regain custody of her child. Somehow, someway, he would accomplish that task in the remaining time he had left as a soldier.

Once they arrived at Nina's cottage, the injured man tried to climb from the back of the wagon and fell to the ground. Jacob rushed to his side. "Let me help you."

"Much obliged."

Jacob helped him inside where the doctor sat at the table, enjoying a cup of coffee. Jacob hoped there was more. He needed it. He laid Herbert on the closest bunk and stepped aside so the doctor could help him. Agnes handed him a cup of coffee and waved him to a chair at the table.

"Please, sit, Mary." He motioned for her to take the seat beside him. "Tell me what happened this morning."

"Barton wasn't there. What you gave me wasn't enough." She shook her head, fear clouding her eyes. "I can't do what they want of me. I can't."

"You won't have to. I'll figure something out."

"So will I." Nina placed a hand on her shoulder. "We'll get your child back."

"You aren't getting involved." Jacob set his cup on the table with enough force to slosh the liquid over the rim.

"I'm already involved. That goon thinks I took his picture."

"Did you?"

She shrugged. "Yes, but—"

Jacob slammed back his chair and stormed outside. How was he going to protect Nina when she placed herself in danger every time he turned around? He rubbed his hands roughly over his face. He was going to fail her, same as he had failed his family.

"He'll be fine," the doctor said, joining him outside. "But he will require some care."

"He will get plenty of that here. These women love to take in those in need," Jacob said.

"Good. I'll check him in a day or two. Thank you for the food. The missus will be pleased."

Jacob nodded. Food and water was almost as valuable as money nowadays. He took a deep breath and reentered the cottage.

Herbert sat up, a white bandage around his midsection. "I've got some broken ribs, the doc said."

"Want to tell me what happened?" Jacob pulled up a chair, spun it around and straddled the wooden seat.

"I've been making amends, the best I can, to atone for my deception. Some folks don't take too kindly to what I did."

"They need to be reported. Can you identify them?"

Herbert exhaled sharply. "Considering they were hired to perform the beating, and not the actual ones I lied to, I'd be happy to tell you who they are."

"And you will remain here while you recover," Nina said. "I insist. We'll pitch a tent for you out front."

"Much obliged."

Jacob had known Nina would offer to help Herbert recuperate, but hearing her say the words rankled. "I'll find the tent." He left the cottage as if it were on fire and practically ran to Fort Mason.

Captain Walker sat behind his desk signing forms. Upon seeing Jacob, he waved him in. "Just the person I wanted to see."

"Yes, sir?" Jacob sat across from him. "I have things that require your attention also."

"You first, Sergeant." Walker laid his pen on top of the stack of papers in front of him.

Jacob spent the next ten minutes telling him of Barton's thievery, prostitution ring and Herbert's beating. "I have a plan to catch the culprits," he said, "but we will require the assistance of the military police." He filled the sergeant in on all that had transpired over the past few days.

The captain nodded, then picked up the top sheet of paper from the stack in front of him. "No need. We will handle things from here. All I need is your signature on your release forms, and you are a civilian once again." He grinned and held out the pen and paper. "Your services will be missed. Unfortunately, there aren't enough soldiers like you."

Jacob stared at the form in front of him. The day had

finally arrived, and early. He signed his signature and stood, saluting his commanding officer for the last time. "I will move my things to an empty tent immediately, sir, and would like to request a tent for an injured man who needs care."

"That we can do."

Jacob wrote down where to send the tent.

"Are you heading back to Kansas any time soon?"

"I haven't decided."

He laughed. "Ah, there must be a woman in the picture. Only a woman can cloud a man's mind so."

Jacob smiled. "There could be, if I can ever figure out what I need to do."

Walker laughed. "Good luck with that."

After ten years, Jacob was a civilian again. The absence of rank rested on his shoulders like a new, uncomfortable shirt. What would he do until he decided his future? He wasn't used to not having orders to lead him through each day. He decided to wander the city with the eyes of a non-military man. He could always offer his help in the daily cleanup efforts. The backbreaking work would be rewarding and would give him time to decide whether to return permanently to his farm or not.

Jacob headed for his tent and packed up his few belongings. Soon, another soldier would lay his head on the pillow. Set his boots under the cot. Jacob shook off his musings and headed for a tent that had been emptied of its occupants the day before. He was tempted to rent one of the cottages, but was reluctant to take what a family could use more.

Thankfully, the tent's prior occupants had left behind a couple of crates. He placed his belongings inside and set off to find someone willing to sell a cot and bedding. Things had certainly changed for him.

What would Nina say when he told her he was no longer enlisted in the service? Would she be happy for him?

As the sun set, he headed for the beach, confident the man he had purchased a bed from would deliver without Jacob's supervision. The man was a bona-fide pastor, after all, not a swindler as Herbert had been. Jacob had also made an appointment with the pastor for tomorrow. It was time for Jacob to deal with matters regarding God.

He shed his shoes, leaving them on the sand, and headed for the water's edge. No longer worrying about damage to his uniform, he stepped into the surf and held his arms wide. He closed his eyes and implored God to speak to him, whether at that moment or on the morrow during his meeting. Jacob needed to settle his future, both physical and spiritual.

Seagulls soared overhead, their feathers tinted with pink from the sunset. Their cries filled the air. Chest heavy, Jacob stepped out of the water.

A woman strolled toward him, her face in shadow. Not Nina, but his foolish heart had leaped for a moment, thinking it could be. Did she come to the beach anymore or had Jacob ruined that pleasure for her?

He put his shoes on and headed for the loneliness of his tent, purchasing a meat pastry on the way. He missed more than the regular walks on the beach with Nina. He missed sharing her dinnertime, her smile, the trusting way she would slip her small hand into his larger one.

He wouldn't give up trying to win her heart. He refused to believe all chances were gone. He would visit with the pastor tomorrow, make his decision and hopefully, possibly, begin to court Nina.

Chapter 14

"Did you pay the rent?" Nina popped her head into Herbert's tent the next morning and stared down at him.

He struggled to a sitting position. "No, why? I can if you need me to. In fact, I should have suggested it sooner."

She waved off his offer. "Then who…?"

Oh, Jacob. Jacob needed to stop helping her. He would be gone soon, and her heart dropped at the thought. She needed to be able to support herself and the others. Not to mention the importance of finding a way to develop her photographs by herself. The sooner she could do that, the sooner she could possibly find a home for Sally.

Passing a large, grand house for sale, she allowed herself a moment to dream of the home filled with children, and possibly a darkroom for her photo developing. She snapped a picture of the house to file away as a remote future possibility. Perhaps she could ask for funds from wealthy people back east who would be glad to support an orphanage. But, first things first.

Soon, she stood outside Jacob's tent. "Hello? Jacob?"

A stranger in military uniform stepped from the tent. "Are you looking for Jacob Taft?"

"Yes." She peered around him.

"He's been discharged, ma'am. I'm new and don't know which tent is his."

"But he's still here in the camp?"

"To my knowledge, yes."

"Thank you." Nina set off at a fast pace through the tents, hoping to spot Jacob. What would she say to him? Would he stay if she asked? Could she form a life with a man whose heart didn't seem right with God? She could try, maybe.

Her steps faltered. No, it went against everything she believed in, but, she also believed in hope. If Jacob chose to stay in San Francisco, they had time. There was hope.

Hope faded as she went up one row and down another with no sight of Jacob. Maybe the other soldier had been mistaken. It was quite possible Jacob had boarded the next train and immediately left for Kansas. He wouldn't have left without saying goodbye, surely.

She spotted Mary walking between the tents. Should she follow her or hunt for Jacob? She could do both. If Jacob were still in camp, she couldn't imagine him stepping aside and not going through with his promise to help Mary. She was certain he would see things through before leaving. By following Mary, she might run into Jacob.

This time, she was more careful not to be seen as Mary approached Barton's tent, her hands empty. The same large man guarded the entrance, not allowing Mary access. Instead, a short, slim man with dark hair came outside. Could this be Barton? Nina snapped his picture.

The man slapped Mary across the face. Her head whipped to the side. She implored him to have mercy, saying she would do better.

Since Mary had nothing to offer the man, Jacob must truly be gone. What could Nina do to spare her friend a horrible fate? She thought of her few belongings. She had so little to spare. Fingering the empty roll of film in her pocket, she came up with a plan.

Johnny came around the corner of the tent, took one

look at the men and Mary, and sprinted in Nina's direction, his dog yapping and running after him. The big man took off after the two of them. When Johnny came close to Nina's hiding spot, she grabbed his arm and yanked him into the trees.

"You know these people." She shook him. "Don't deny it. Why would you run otherwise?"

"I heard a rumor they had left the camp. I thought I was safe going down that row." He pulled free, his face pale. "The little man is Barton. He wants me to give him half of my rat money. I can't do that. We need the money, Miss Hansen. Some other boy hunts rats at the Presidio."

"I know we do. I'm sorry I shook you, but you scared ten years off my life. Stay away from that part of camp."

A crashing through the trees sent her and Johnny racing for home. "What else have you heard?" She asked when they stopped to catch their breath.

"I'm catching as many rats as I can, but there are too many. People are taking sick and crying that it's the black plague."

Bubonic? Her blood chilled. "Come on. We have to get home. We'll talk more there."

By the time they arrived at the cottage, Nina's side ached and her breath came in gasps. She burst through the door, after Jimmy, and bolted it closed. She leaned against the wood and struggled to catch her breath.

"What happened?" Agnes pulled Ethan close to her side.

"Mary is in trouble and so, I fear, are we." Nina plopped into a chair at the table beside Herbert.

"What can I do?" he asked.

"Nothing, in your condition." Nina put her head in her hands. There wasn't anything anyone could do. Their hope had been in Jacob. With his discharge, had he been around, she doubted even he could help them now.

She wasn't as strong as she had thought she was. She considered herself brave, if not a bit foolhardy at times, but this was all beyond her. She needed help. She needed Jacob.

"What happened to Mary?" Agnes sat across from Nina.

"She didn't have anything to give the crime boss, and he hit her. Then, the man turned on Johnny." She gave the boy a small smile. "It's a good thing Johnny is a fine runner. Although, I fear we might have been followed despite our attempts at avoiding our pursuer."

"You were chased?" Herbert struggled to his feet. "Perhaps if I spoke to the man…offered him money to release Mary from his hands."

"I doubt that would work."

A banging on the door caused everyone to jump to their feet. Herbert peered out the small window. "It's Mary, and she seems to be alone." He unbolted the door, pulled the woman inside, then locked it again.

"You poor thing." Agnes poured her a cup of coffee. "It's weak, we're almost out, but it should put some color back in your cheeks."

Mary fell onto her bunk. The left side of her face still showed Barton's handprint. "I went to Mr. Jacob's tent this morning, to get the things I would need to give to Mr. Barton, but he wasn't there." Tears streaked her face. "I had to go empty-handed. Where is he, Nina?"

"Discharged."

"So, he's gone." She covered her face and sobbed. "My baby is lost to me forever."

"I have a plan." Nina slipped her hand into her pocket. "Barton knows I've been snapping pictures and possibly believes I have taken one of him. This is a blank film, but unless he has a way of developing it, which I doubt, you can take it to him. You can tell him that you live with me and heard me talking of what I had done, but that your first allegiance is with him. Then, give him the film."

"That might work," Herbert said. "You need stipulations, though. He only gets the film if he releases the hold he has on you and your daughter. Hide the film and tell him you'll retrieve it if he agrees."

"Why don't we go to the police?" Agnes asked.

"Jacob said he told his commanding officer." Nina accepted a cup of the weak coffee from Agnes, making a mental note to purchase more. "I fear the army will be too slow to help Mary."

"If I go to the police," Mary said. "Mr. Barton will kill me and my little girl. He has said as much, and I believe him."

Nina believed him, too. "We'll turn in the film and pray it is enough." It had to be.

She moved to the window. A slight breeze rustled the tree branches. She wanted to sit outside as she usually did and enjoy watching people go about their daily lives. But it was no longer safe. Not only because of Barton, but because of the rumor Johnny had mentioned. Could there really be bubonic plague in the camps?

How was it spread? She knew the cause had something to do with rats. "Johnny, I'm afraid you have to stop hunting for rats. I also need you to burn your clothes, and wash yourself and your dog. Agnes, we need to scrub every inch of this cottage. Johnny told me there is possibly plague in the camps. We need to keep ourselves from becoming sick and to rid the camp of filth, both two- and four-legged."

Jacob rapped on the cottage at the edge of the Presidio camp. Seconds later, an elderly man in a faded dark suit answered the door. "Pastor Rodwell?"

"Yes." The man squinted behind wire-rimmed glasses. "Oh, it's you, Mr. Taft. I hope the cot is sufficient for your needs."

"It is. Thank you. I need some counsel, sir. I can pay you." Jacob needed to find Nina, but wanted some things settled first.

"No payment is necessary." Pastor Rodwell stepped aside and ushered Jacob in. "I've always time for someone searching for truth."

With both of the small windows open, the interior was a few degrees cooler than outside. A welcome relief. Jacob had made his last round of the Golden Gate camp, relieved to not see Mary, or Nina, outside Barton's tent. Now, with the dinner hour approaching, he wanted to settle his spiritual matter so he could take a box of food supplies to Nina and her "family." More than anything, he wanted to declare his feelings for her and offer his help wherever it was needed. If he were honest, he wouldn't mind a hug from the sweet little Sally again, either.

Pastor Rodwell took a seat at a small table and motioned for Jacob to do the same. "Now, how may I help? A glass of water, perhaps?" He motioned a plump woman who knitted in the corner to come over. "I'm afraid we're out of coffee. This is my dear wife, Ingrid."

"Pleased to meet you, ma'am." He set the box he carried on the table and withdrew one of the two cans of coffee. "I've extra. Please, take this."

The pastor's eyes widened. "I said no payment was necessary, but I am weak enough to accept this gift. Thank you." He took the can and handed it to his wife who immediately bustled to the stove where a pot sat.

He turned back to Jacob. "Now, what can I do for you?"

Jacob stared at his hands. Where to begin to tell this man of the burden he had carried for almost fifteen years? The scars that kept him from telling Nina that he loved her.

"When I was fifteen, my family home caught fire." Jacob clenched his hands on the table hard enough to turn the knuckles white. The scars on his back burned as if they were fresh. "My father shoved me out first, then turned back to get my mother and sister. We fought. I wanted to help." He choked back a sob. "A burning beam landed across my shoulders. My father dragged me outside, then ran back in. The roof caved and fell. They were…all lost."

"You've thought the death of your family to be your fault? That is a heavy burden for one so young to carry."

Jacob nodded. "It has kept me from allowing anyone to get close to me. I've been lonely for as long as I can remember."

"And blaming God, if I'm correct."

"Yes, sir. I'm ready to let all of that go."

"Is a woman the cause of your change of heart?"

Jacob laughed, the sound without humor. "A woman who collects lost people like one would collect shiny pennies."

The pastor returned his smile. "Where is this woman now?"

"Running herself ragged helping everyone who crosses her path." He held out his cup for Mrs. Rodwell to fill with hot brew. "I've not gone to church or opened a Bible in years. I'd like you to help remedy that." He didn't count the services he had endured listening to Herbert preach the same thing over and over. Though some of it had sunk in. It was time for Jacob to give up the fight and place it in the hands of someone who could handle it.

"What if we study together every Monday, Wednesday and Friday evening until the truth is made clear?" The pastor steepled his fingers, his eyes twinkling. "Your girl is a woman of faith, is she not?"

"Very much so." Jacob finished his coffee and stood. "Speaking of my girl, I want to drop this box of food off at her place. She has several mouths to feed."

Pastor Rodwell pulled a Bible from a crate next to the bed. "Take this. Read it. Bring any questions that arise to me at our next meeting. Go with God, son."

Jacob nodded, staring at the book in his hand as if it was the last Bible on earth. He set the book in the box of food and hefted it in his arms. "I'm still able to get things that are hard for others. Let me know if you need anything."

Pastor Rodwell escorted him to the door. "If you can get your hands on a couple of potatoes, I'd be much obliged. The wife has a yearning for one."

"I think I can manage that."

Jacob strolled through camp, mulling over his conversation with the pastor. The aromas of meals being cooked teased his stomach, reminding him that he had missed lunch.

He stopped in front of Nina's cottage, surprised at not seeing her sitting outside as was her custom. He prayed, yes, prayed for the first time in years that nothing was wrong. Shifting the box to one arm, he knocked.

"Jacob?" Nina whipped open the door. Her eyes were red. "I thought you had gone."

"Without saying goodbye?" What must she think of him? "I've brought you food."

"Did you pay my rent?"

"Yes." He frowned. "May I come in?"

"Of course, but, Jacob, you've got to stop. I need to care for my own." She let him in and slid the bolt.

"Why are you locked inside?"

She glanced at Herbert, who reclined on the bottom

bunk, his eyes closed, then at Mary. "We've had some… trouble."

He dropped the box on the table. "Oh, Mary." The mark on her face was his fault as much as if he had struck her. "What happened?"

They all started talking at once. Sally tugged on his shirttail. He scooped her up. "Nina, you explain."

Nina told him of following Mary, running away with Johnny, her plan, and fears of the plague. So that explained the odor of soap coming from the pot on the stove. It would take them forever to wash all their things on the stove. Wait. She had followed Mary?

"Barton knows where you live?" He shook his head and sat heavily in the nearest chair. "The film idea might work, but it is a risk." How could he convince Nina to stay away from danger? He tightened his hold on Sally. The children needed her. *He* needed her.

"What about the army? Mary, have you seen them around Barton's tent?"

"No, sir. They must be too busy with other things to care about a crook."

They would get around to investigating, but it might not be in time for Mary or Nina. "I can try again." He wrinkled his nose as the odor of lye soap grew stronger. "We need to open the windows. Tomorrow, I will bring you a washbasin."

Nina sighed. "I can purchase one myself."

"Why? I want to help."

"Let him help." Herbert sat up. "Lord knows I'm worthless. I think speaking with your former commanding officer is a good idea."

"You have no say in this." Nina planted her hands on her hips. Jacob's heart leaped. He started setting cans of food on the table to hide his grin. Soon, he would be the type of man Nina wanted. The type of man she deserved.

"I give up," Nina said. "I can't argue with both of you."

"Good," Jacob and Herbert said in unison.

Agnes grabbed two cans of stewed meat. "I'll fix dinner. Someone open the front door. No one will bother us with Mr. Taft here."

Jacob hoped so, but he couldn't be there around the clock. He needed to find a way to stop Barton before anyone was hurt. New Bible study or not, he would blame himself if anything happened to anyone under Nina's roof. What was taking Captain Walker so long?

"Is this a Bible?" Nina held up the book.

"Yes." He took it from her and put it back in the box. "It's mine."

She shrieked and threw her arms around his neck. "Finally."

He returned her hug, a grin spreading across his face.

Chapter 15

"I don't feel so good, Miss Hansen." Johnny leaned against the outside of the cottage a week later.

Nina placed the back of her hand against his forehead. "You're burning up. Here, sit down." She led him to a stool. "Wait here." Her heart beat in her throat. The cries of plague had rang through the camp for days, tainting the air with fear and hysteria. *Please, God, don't let Johnny have it.* "Agnes," she said, entering the house. "Johnny is outside, and ill. I need to find a place to nurse him without endangering the rest of you."

"Is it the plague?" She put her hands over her heart.

"I don't know. Where is Mary?"

Agnes shrugged. "She was gone when I woke. Took your last roll of film, too."

Nina sighed. She hadn't wanted the other woman to deliver the film without protection, and they were still waiting for Captain Walker to send help. "I need to find Jacob."

"Use my tent at the other camp," Herbert said from his seat at the table. "If he's ill, you don't want to endanger his younger brother. You know Sam follows Johnny everywhere he's allowed. I had planned on returning to it today, but if it's needed, and you don't mind my company beside your front door for a few more days, you're welcome to it."

"Bless you." Nina laid a quick kiss on his cheek. "Please

have someone deliver medical supplies to me as soon as possible."

She returned to Johnny. "Put your arm around my shoulder." Hopefully, they could find a wagon willing to take them to the other park.

"What if it's the plague?" Tears welled in his eyes. "I don't want you to take ill."

"Don't worry about me. It isn't the plague. I won't let it be." She struggled under his weight. Nina wasn't petite in form, but her slender build was no match for a growing young man.

Slow, but steady, they exited the camp entrance. A wagon rumbled by. Nina called out for the driver to stop. He took one look at Johnny and continued on his way. No matter. Another would be by soon. They continued their slow process down the streets of San Francisco, each wagon they came across refusing to give them a ride because of the risk of sickness.

Nina's feet and back ached. She made Johnny sit on a pile of scaffolding. She had seen little of Jacob this past week. He had told her he was studying the Bible with a pastor. This was a moment when Nina would have welcomed his help.

After resting for a few minutes, she again thrust her shoulder under Johnny's arm. Her hair had fallen from its bun and stuck to her face and neck with perspiration. Johnny's skin burned through his shirt and her blouse, making her hot.

Where was the ocean breeze? She lifted her head, trying to catch any wind that might blow past.

"Let me walk on my own," Johnny said. "I'm too heavy."

"No. You're much too weak."

They struggled on. Nina exhaled in relief when she

saw the Golden Gate Park sign. Now, to get Johnny to Herbert's tent.

"Nina?" Jacob rushed toward them. "What's happened?"

"I'm taking Johnny to Herbert's tent. He's ill, and I don't want him around the others."

"You've brought him this far alone? Why didn't you send someone for me?" He took over the burden of Johnny and headed to Herbert's tent, Nina following.

"I was afraid there wasn't time to send someone, wait for you to return, then come here. No wagon would give us a ride." She ducked into the tent. "Do you think it's the plague?"

"Possibly. There is a suspected outbreak and our brave lad had been hunting the rats daily." He met Nina's gaze.

"Where did it start?"

"No one knows where it started."

Johnny cried out. "Help me, Miss Hansen."

"I won't leave your side." She smoothed his dark hair away from his eyes. "Jacob, would it be too much of a bother to ask you to fetch some cool water? We need to break his fever."

"I'll get barrels of seawater. It's cool enough."

Nina felt helpless. Other than keeping Johnny as comfortable as possible, there was little she could do. She threw his shirt and pants in the fire pit outside the tent. While she waited for Jacob, she set fire to the clothes, then scrounged up something of Herbert's for the boy to wear.

What little she knew of the plague told her the disease was transmitted by fleas, and she prayed Agnes would, once again, scour the cottage. Nina headed back into the tent.

When Jacob arrived an hour later with two pails of

water, he had changed his clothes. Good. One less thing for Nina to worry about.

"There is a barrel of fresh water coming. I was able to send someone to the Presidio for it. I will find you something clean to wear."

Nina spent her time waiting by continuously wiping Johnny's face, arms and neck with the cool water. When the rag grew warm, she swirled it in the air to cool it, then mopped his face again.

She would need to mark the tent quarantined, if Jacob hadn't done so already.

"Nina?" Jacob called from outside, then stuck his arm through the opening. "This should fit you fairly well. It's freshly laundered."

"Thank you."

The faded green dress was a bit short and too big in the bosom, but would preserve her modesty. "You may come in."

"How is he doing?" Jacob's brow creased as he looked down at Johnny. "Would you like me to check on the rest of your family?"

His questions warmed her. When had he realized that the others were, indeed, her family? "He's bad, I think, and yes, if you could make sure they've properly cleaned the cottage and bathed, I will be forever grateful. If anyone else has taken ill, please bring them to me."

He nodded. "I'll bring you something to eat when I return." He cupped her cheek. "Don't overexert yourself. I couldn't handle it if you took ill, too."

She leaned into his touch. "I'll be careful."

"I've put a black *X* on the tent. Don't go outside unless you have to. I don't want the other residents to bother you."

"I won't." Although the inside of the tent was stifling, and a walk along the beach sounded wonderful, she would stay inside. If some frightened person were to assault her, hurt her in some way, she wouldn't be able to care for Johnny.

She resumed her task of fighting his fever, wishing she knew more about the deadly plague. While she dribbled water into his mouth and washed his face, she prayed.

Soon, exhaustion slowed her efforts. That, combined with the heat in the tent, had her eyelids growing heavy. She rested her head on the mattress. A short nap would do wonders. If she were refreshed, she could do more good for the sick boy than if she could barely stand up herself.

She needed someone to work in shifts with her if he was sick for any length of time. Dare she ask Jacob? He would, if she asked, but she knew he spent his days in helping reconstruct the city. Who needed him more, her or the fallen San Francisco?

Cleaning was under full attack when Jacob arrived at Nina's cottage an hour later. The youngest children played in the shade of a tree. Jacob rushed forward and helped Herbert wrestle a mattress through the door. "I'm not sure you should be doing this kind of labor yet. Are the ribs healed well enough?"

"Passable." Herbert shrugged. "Someone has to. Agnes can't do it alone." He smiled over Jacob's shoulder.

So, it was like that now. Good. Now that Herbert had done his best to turn from his life of lying, he could be just the man for Agnes.

"How are Johnny and Nina?" Agnes dumped blankets into a washtub of boiling water, then swiped her hand across her brow. "Nina wants her medicine box," Jacob told her.

"Let me get it. There isn't much in there to help if it is the plague, but maybe some peppermint tea will help

Johnny." Agnes went into the cottage and returned, holding a small wood box with a handle. "There are some oils in there that might help relieve his suffering."

"Thank you. Anyone else feeling ill?" He took the box and glanced at the children.

"Not so far."

Thank God. Jacob headed back to help Nina.

After seeing her with Johnny, he had gone straight to his former commanding officer and asked for a barrel of fresh water, explaining the ease of quarantine if no one needed to leave the infected area. Captain Walker had agreed.

Jacob had also asked what was happening with the charges against Barton and had been told in a polite but firm manner that it was being handled and was no longer any of his concern. He disagreed, since he doubted whether the danger to Nina had lessened, and he considered her his concern. Also hanging over the current dangers was the ever present thought of what to do about his land in Kansas.

He had an idea of what his final decision would be, but what if Nina didn't agree? He shook his head. He'd worry about that later.

When he returned to Nina and Johnny, Mary stood outside the tent with Nina. What were those two up to now?

"I gave Mr. Barton's man the film," Mary said. "And he said he knew someone who could develop it while Mr. Barton is out of town. What are we going to do now?"

Nina paled. "I'll think of something."

"No, you won't." Jacob handed her the box. "The two of you will stay as far away from that man as possible." He had no idea what he was going to do about the increased danger.

"Mr. Taft, sir." The sergeant who had taken his place

as main overseer of the camp ran to his side and handed him a telegraph.

"Thank you." Jacob read the note. Someone wanted to buy his family land in Kansas. Did he want to sell? Maybe. He needed to make a trip back. If he did, his heart would tell him where he belonged.

"Is it bad news?" Nina placed a hand on his arm, then jumped back as if he was on fire. "I'm so sorry. If you get sick—"

"It won't have anything to do with you touching me. I seriously doubt Johnny has the plague. That was wiped out before the earthquake." He folded the message and slid it into his pocket. "I need to go to Kansas."

"Now?" She frowned. "I need you."

He glanced at Mary, who scuttled away. "We can't begin to think of a possible future unless I square things away back there. I can't do anything more for Johnny than you can. You'll be fine. Just promise me that you will stay away from Barton and let Captain Walker handle this. If I don't go now, the buyer may change his mind. I might not get another opportunity."

She nodded. "I promise. But once he develops that film, he will know he's been swindled."

"Captain Walker said he is handling it. If something feels wrong, or you feel as if you are in danger, go to him. He'll help you."

She nodded, her eyes shimmering with unshed tears. "Are you coming back?"

"Yes. I promise." He took the liberty of kissing her, wanting to take the feel and smell of her with him. She kissed him back, pressing close. He tasted her tears, hating to leave her, but he couldn't have a future without taking care of the past.

He caressed her cheek, then left, his decision about his land already made.

Two hours later, Jacob climbed onto a crowded railroad car and settled into a seat between two very large men in suits who proceeded to talk about their wealth in loud voices. He hoped they tooted their own horns because they were donating to help the victims in San Francisco. He closed his eyes and tried to sleep.

As the men continued to discuss their business, Jacob squirmed, trying to get comfortable and let them know, without having to say anything, that he wanted to rest. They didn't catch his hint. Jacob sighed and opened his eyes. It was going to be a very long trip.

By the time he arrived in Kansas, Jacob was disheveled, sleep deprived, cranky and missing Nina. He couldn't wait to arrive back in San Francisco with her surprise. He prayed she would be as happy to receive what he wanted to give her as he was to give it.

After three days on the train, and not sparing his rude train ride companions a second look, Jacob grabbed his duffel bag and headed for the nearest hotel and restaurant. He had two hours before meeting the potential buyer at the bank, and it had been a long time since the apple he had eaten for breakfast.

He checked in to the hotel, left his bag at the front desk and headed immediately to the restaurant. Admiring the white linens and crystal goblets, he wondered whether Nina would enjoy such a fancy place. He smiled. She would most likely prefer a picnic on the beach.

"Jacob Taft?"

He turned and grinned, recognizing an old friend of his father's. "Mr. Harrison." He thrust out his hand.

"None of that, my boy." The older man wrapped him in a hug. "You're out of uniform."

Jacob nodded. "My enlistment is up. I've come home to settle some business."

"Oh?" He waved Jacob into the empty seat at his table. "Do you plan on staying?"

"Actually, I'm here to sell the home place. I'm meeting a buyer soon."

"Absolutely not." Mr. Harrison narrowed his eyes. "I've been keeping the place up. Your father promised me first opportunity if the land and house should ever sell. I'll pay more than the fair asking price."

"There is no one I would want to sell it to more." Jacob grinned. "After a bite to eat, I'd like to ride out there and take one last look."

"It won't be your last look," Mr. Harrison said, smiling. "You come and visit often. Make sure you bring with you whatever woman has stolen your heart out there in California. I can't think of another reason why you would stay there." He took a sip of water from his goblet. "Me and the missus were mighty worried about you after hearing about that quake. I'm glad to see you still breathing."

"Me, too, but there is still a lot to be done before the city resembles any of its former beauty." Now, knowing of no better buyer than a family friend, Jacob could take a late train that very day and head back to Nina.

The thought of her battling both a devastating disease and threats from a madman left his blood cold. He wanted things wrapped up that day.

Once they had finished eating a quick dinner, Jacob rode in Mr. Harrison's truck ten miles out of town. They drove down a long dirt driveway and stopped in front of his two-story, whitewashed farmhouse. He had hoped, once, that Nina might have considered moving to Kansas, but he knew now that many children had been left orphaned by the quake. She was needed there, not in Kansas as a farmer's wife.

He took a deep breath against thoughts of nostalgia. Perhaps, they could one day bring all the children in her care out here for a vacation. "Let's go to the bank. I need to let the other party know you're purchasing the land, and get the paperwork started to transfer the deed to you."

Mr. Harrison nodded. "I'll still be living at my place, but I need the land and water for my cattle. Don't worry. I'll keep the place ready for when you visit. What do you want the money for?"

Jacob told him about the house for sale. "Nina, that's the woman I want to marry, would like nothing more than to run an orphanage. I aim to help her."

"Why didn't you say so? There's no need to sell your land. I'll rent it from you. Your military pension should cover the cost of the California house. If not, use this place as collateral for a loan. No need at all to sell the home place, much as I'd like to buy it."

He was right. It wasn't until that moment that Jacob realized how much he loved the farm and its house. As much as he also loved Nina, he was happy not to have to part with it. "It's a deal. You are now the prime renter of a nice chunk of acreage."

They laughed and shook hands. Jacob couldn't wait to head back to Nina and tell her of his plans.

Chapter 16

"Someone stole little Sally's dress off the clothesline." Agnes slammed the laundry basket on the table. "Yesterday, it was the stew, right off the fire! This crime has to stop."

"Desperate times create desperate people." Nina set aside her mending of Sam's pants. When Johnny had woken that morning with no more signs of illness, she had chalked his sickness to something he had eaten or perhaps influenza. She had given thanks many times over. Herbert had returned to his tent in the other camp. "But, I agree something has to be done."

The inkling of an idea formed in her mind. Anytime anyone had something important to say, they stood on a crate in the common area and gave their views on a large variety of subjects. Nina would speak on the rash of crime within the camps and ask the refugees to band together. No one had seen hide nor hair of Barton recently. If she wanted to make her speech, it had to be now.

She glanced around the cottage. Another young girl, Sarah, had been added to their midst yesterday, a child around the age of twelve. Nina needed to find larger lodgings. Mary had already left for the day, no doubt returning to her life of thievery to keep Barton from harming her, and Johnny, despite Nina's objections, had returned to catching rats. She had told him emphatically to get rid of the things before coming home each day.

She shuddered. They were lucky this time that the plague hadn't darkened their door, but how long could they be spared? Sure, Johnny's hunting brought in much-needed income, but at what cost?

"When is Jacob coming back?" Agnes folded the laundry, setting the clothes in neat piles on the table. "He could put a stop to this stealing. That man finds a way to do anything."

Nina grinned. "I thought you were sweet on Herbert?"

"I am, but I know a good man when I see one, and how much you miss him shows on your face."

True. Her missing Jacob was a constant ache. He had said his travel would take only a few days. Five days had passed. Not enough to worry, things happened to thwart even the best-laid plans, but Nina missed him fiercely. She even missed his grumpy face when she did something he thought too dangerous. Smiling, she stood and headed into the coolness of the day. Late summer would soon give way to autumn.

She sat on a stool and twirled a stick in the newly doused fire. She glanced at the empty clotheslines strung between the cottage and a sturdy tree. Making a speech about the local crime might not do as much good as she hoped, but she needed to keep her mind occupied until Jacob returned.

Her heart warmed at the thought of him and his regular Bible studies. The two of them hadn't spoken of what went on during his studies, but there was a subtle softening in the rigid lines of Jacob's shoulders. She prayed it mirrored a softening of his heart.

"Good morning, Nina." Herbert approached, smiling at her. "Is Agnes home? I've managed to get my hands on some canned preserves."

"Another gift?" Nina smiled back. "Your offerings benefit us all."

He sighed. "I had a loaf of fresh-baked bread, but some scoundrel grabbed it right from my hands. A young lad around your Johnny's age." He shrugged. "Obviously, the boy needed it worse than we do."

"We've lost some things, too." Nina would give her plea at the Presidio camp and then make her way to repeat it at Golden Gate Park. Perhaps her late afternoon and early evening would be too busy for her to dwell on Jacob's absence.

She smoothed her skirts. No time like the present. She patted her pocket with the film that contained a photo of Sally and one of Barton. She hoped to find a developer operating somewhere in the city. She ducked inside the cottage long enough to grab a biscuit with strawberry preserves, then set out on her mission.

Her speech at the Presidio went well, punctuated with cries of "Amen" and "yes." Feeling as if things might change in the camp, she set off through the city.

A group of men hammered panels of wood over the windows of a newly built building. "Excuse me." Nina approached them, staying well out of reach in case they decided a woman on her own was easy prey.

A middle-aged man turned with a grin. "Hello."

"I'm wondering, if during your trips through the city, you might know of a place I could get film developed?" More and more places of business opened each day, so she was hopeful.

"Sure. There's a camera place two streets over on the north side." He gave her a nod and returned to work.

"Thank you." Nina increased her pace, arriving in front of a building that smelled strongly of pine and paint. She took a deep breath and pushed inside, surprised to see that the man behind the counter was the same man who had given her the film on the day of the quake. "You made it through."

"As did you." He grinned, completely sober this time. "How did the camera work for you? Did you have enough film?"

"It's all wonderful. Would you like payment?"

He shook his head. "No, it was a gift. I never thought I could rebuild, but companies back east are funding small businesses to reopen. What can I do for you?"

She pulled the film from her pocket. "Can you develop this?"

"I sure can. I'll have it ready for you in the morning."

Nina thrust out her hand. "You're a blessing."

"I'm not sure about that, but I do know it pleases me to see you alive and well."

Smiling, Nina exited the shop and continued to Golden Gate Park. If all went well, Sally could have a permanent family by Christmas, not to mention their latest addition, Sarah. Nina's heart swelled. Things were definitely looking up.

When she reached the camp's common area, she listened to a woman promoting her laundry business to the crowd. After the woman finished, Nina stepped onto the crate and waited for the crowd to settle.

When all eyes were on her, she spoke. "Ladies and gentlemen, I come before you with a request that will benefit us all. As many of you have no doubt experienced, thievery and debauchery runs rampant through the refugee camps."

"What do you aim to do about it, little lady?" a man shouted from the crowd. "You got a thief right in your own home."

"Well, sir, I propose we all work together to run the unsavory characters out of the camp. Mary has changed her ways, believe me. In addition to not frequenting their establishments or buying stolen goods, I suggest we also report any nefarious activities to the police."

"The police haven't helped us much yet," a woman called out.

"I agree that law enforcement is sadly overworked, but even alerting the sergeant in charge of the camp is a wonderful start."

"I say we take the law into our own hands!"

"Yes!"

"A vigilante committee!"

"No, wait." Nina held up her hands. "That isn't what I'm proposing at all. Please, listen to me. We all want our children to grow up in a safe place. A place with morals. A place where they are free to play in the parks without us parents worrying that some evil may befall them. If we work together, under the law, we can accomplish this. I implore you all to keep a sharp eye on what happens around you and report anything unlawful. Together, we can do this."

Applause broke out as she jumped from the crate. Her cheeks ached from grinning and her back stung from well-meaning claps on her shoulders. A job well done, if she said so herself.

With the sun beginning its descent over the horizon, Nina headed for home.

"Nice little speech, girlie." The man who usually stood guard outside Barton's tent grabbed her elbow.

"Let go of me!" She tried to yank free, but his grip tightened.

"I think not. You're coming with me."

"I will not." She aimed a kick at his shin.

The man slammed his fist into her jaw, knocking her to the ground. She blinked up at him through multicolored stars. The last thing she noticed before losing consciousness was that the man missed a tooth.

Jacob stepped off the train and into a cool, autumn, San Francisco morning. His train had been delayed thanks to a tree falling across the tracks. It had taken hours to clear away the debris. He took a deep breath of the salt-laden air and headed directly for Nina's cottage.

He rapped sharply on the door and was greeted by a harried-looking Agnes.

"Oh, sir, I had hoped you were Nina."

His heart dropped. "What has happened?"

She held the door wide and ushered him inside. "She went to implore the camps to pay heed and try to stop the rash of crime growing. She hasn't returned. We haven't seen her since yesterday afternoon. Mary didn't return last night, either. I'm worried."

Jacob dropped his duffel on the floor and met the anxious gaze of Herbert. "No one has heard anything?"

"No. Johnny is out scouting for word, but—" His shoulders slumped.

What had Nina been thinking to head out alone? Why had the others allowed her to? "I need to speak to Captain Walker." He found the captain strolling the grounds of the Presidio. "Sir!"

"Mr. Taft? I assumed you had gone back to Kansas."

"I did for a few days, but I've decided to make my home here." Jacob stopped to catch his breath. "I fear two women have been abducted." He told Walker of Nina's last known whereabouts and Mary's disappearance. "Has anything been done in regards to Barton?"

Walker shook his head. "We sent men to arrest him yesterday, but he's moved out. No one knows anything, of course."

Dread slithered through Jacob's veins. "He has the two women, sir, I'm sure of it."

"I'm beginning to think so." He stared into the distance. "Without proof, and knowing the man's whereabouts, there isn't much we can do."

"Can't you send a patrol to search the streets? Surely, someone has seen something."

"I can, and I will. Come with me." They headed for the barracks. Walker slammed through the door, causing men to bolt to attention. "Mr. Taft is no longer enlisted in the army, and I know you men are on a two-day furlough, but we are asking for volunteers to help him locate, under his direction, two women we fear have been kidnapped by a crime lord. Any takers?"

Ten hands shot up. Jacob's legs threatened to give way, so strong was his relief. "I have no other plan than to go building to building in the abandoned sectors of the city. Those of you volunteering, please meet me in the courtyard in fifteen minutes." He turned to Walker. "Thank you."

"I will pray they are found. I would come myself, but I have more duties than I have time." He gave Jacob a nod before heading away.

The fifteen minutes seemed like an hour. But soon the ten men, dressed in military uniform and weapons hanging from their belt, joined Jacob. He gave them his thanks and headed to the outskirts of the city. If Barton were in hiding, he would choose a section of the city that was vacant.

As they marched, he prayed, harder than he had ever prayed before. Peace descended upon him. They would find her. He had no doubt. He only hoped it would be sooner rather than later. What must she be going through at the hands of Barton?

The first building they approached, while leaning to one side, looked as if it would remain upright as they searched.

After all, it had stood in that position since the quake with-out falling.

"Spread out!" Jacob waved the soldiers through the rooms, racing up the stairs to the second floor.

Other than broken furniture and discarded clothing, the rooms were empty. Jacob stared out a window. Would Barton choose a vacant home, a business or a warehouse? Many such buildings contained a basement where it would be easy to hide a captive. Jacob thought a warehouse, but didn't want to rule out the possibility he might be wrong.

Once they declared the building they were in to be va-cant, the men headed to the next one, only to be dealt the same disappointment. Jacob reminded himself it was just the second building, but the search was proving to be time-consuming.

Was Nina in pain? Did she have food or water? What did Barton, if he was in fact her captor, plan on doing with her? The possibilities left his mouth dry and his heart heavy.

By midday, they had searched five buildings with noth-ing to show for their efforts. The soldiers took a break to eat military rations, sharing them with Jacob. The food wasn't foreign to him, but stuck in his throat despite drink-ing half a canteen of water. Taking the time to eat strung his nerves thin. He wanted to keep moving, but couldn't fault the volunteers for wanting a break.

When the men got to their feet, Jacob jumped to his, eager to resume the search. The thought of Nina spend-ing another night as a violent man's captive soured his stomach.

Had Nina run across the man herself or had Mary turned her in to save herself? A mother's love was strong. It was more than possible that Nina had been handed to Barton in exchange for Mary's child. Even more possible that Nina, given her kind heart, had offered herself in exchange. No. He shook his head. She wouldn't leave the children willingly.

He and the others entered yet another dilapidated building and had no more luck than with the others. How long would it take to search a city as large as San Francisco? She had to be here. This area was unburned and the quake had left little damage compared to other parts of the city. She had to be here.

"Sir." A soldier held up a hair ribbon, the blue color bright against the soot-covered walls. "I found this in the middle of the sidewalk. Looks like it might have fallen fairly recently."

Jacob agreed. Nina might not be the only woman who tied their hair into a bun with ribbon, but a woman had passed that way, and not too long ago. He took the ribbon and stuck it in his pocket. They were getting closer. He could feel it. He took a moment to say another prayer, then followed the soldiers into yet another building.

"Movement down the street, sir!" A soldier pointed through a busted window.

Jacob peered out to see someone darting between the buildings and staying to the shadows. Since they hadn't seen anyone all morning, the person needed investigating. "Bring him here, but don't shoot."

Two of the soldiers sprinted out the door and returned a few minutes later with Johnny, his mutt growling and snarling at the soldiers' legs. "What are you doing here, son?" Jacob put his hands on Johnny's shoulders.

"Helping." He scowled at the two men who had dragged him inside. "It's easier for me to scout around pretending to hunt rats than it is for a patrol of soldiers to go unseen."

"Have you found her?"

"Not yet, but I have an idea of where she might be."

Johnny straightened. "I need you to let me go alone and see. I'll return in fifteen minutes with a report."

"It's dangerous."

"I'm hunting rats," Johnny said with a sly grin. "My cover story is better than yours if I get caught."

Jacob scratched his jaw. The boy was right, but if something happened to him, Nina would never forgive him. "All right. You have fifteen minutes. If you aren't back by then, we're all coming after you."

"I'll be back." With a whistle to his dog, the boy dashed out of sight.

Jacob took a swig out of his canteen and leaned against the windowsill to wait. He eyed the pistol in one of the soldier's belt and wished for the one he had turned in upon leaving the army. It was just as well. He didn't want to shoot Barton on sight. Not until he made sure Nina was all right.

"He's coming back, sir." The soldier held the door open for Johnny to run inside.

"I found her." He leaned over to catch his breath. "Her and Mary."

"Tell me what you saw." Jacob handed him the canteen. The boy was soaked with perspiration.

"They're both tied to chairs in the basement of a warehouse. I glanced through a slit in the boards. Miss Hansen looks like she's asleep, but Mary was awake and saw me."

"How many men are guarding them?"

"Two not counting Barton. He was there, smoking in a corner. You could arrest him on that alone, couldn't you?"

Jacob smiled. "Fires aren't forbidden any longer." He clapped Johnny on the shoulder. "You did well, son. Now head home and let the others know. We'll be there with Nina in a couple of hours."

Jacob pulled his hat firmly on his head. *Hold on, Nina. I'm coming.*

Chapter 17

Nina groaned and opened her eyes. Why was she tied to a chair? Oh, now she remembered. Barton's goon had grabbed her on her way home.

Mary sat tied to a chair opposite her. The other woman gave a sad smile. "It will be okay," she whispered. "I saw someone peeking through the basement window. I could only see one eye, but I did see it. Help is coming."

"What does he want with us?" Nina pulled against her bindings. They held tight, cutting off the circulation to her arms.

"He had the film developed." Mary's eyes narrowed. "I told you he would, and then we would be in trouble. He said as much when him and his men left the room while you were sleeping."

Yes, she had said almost those exact words. So much for grand speeches about lowering crime. Here she was, right in the middle of the most dangerous crime against her, and not one of the people who had been in the park knew anything about it. Still, if Mary saw what she thought she saw, they would be fine. Nina closed her eyes again and prayed.

When she didn't return home, Agnes and the others would be worried and go to the authorities. All Nina had to do was wait and ignore her growling stomach.

"How long have we been here?" she asked.

"Since yesterday." Mary shrugged. "I sure would like to see Mr. Taft right about now. No one would bother us with him around."

Nina agreed. She sure would like to see Jacob, too, but not if it meant putting his life in danger. She wasn't concerned with herself, only those who depended on her, and that number was growing every day.

Despite her resolve to be brave, she shrank in her seat when the door opened. Mr. Barton strolled in, hands folded behind his back, and grinned. "You little ladies thought you had a good plan worked out, didn't you? Unfortunately for you, I'm smarter than the both of you combined."

Nina lifted her chin and straightened in her chair. She would not show fear. Mrs. Fox had told her never to show fear. And she hadn't, not once during all her years at being teased for living in an orphanage. Mrs. Fox had told her to hold her head high. She wasn't a mistake. God didn't make mistakes. With that thought, she realized nothing that happened to her could pull her away from Him. Fear had no business in the room.

"How long do you intend to keep us here?" she asked.

"Well, I don't know." Mr. Barton paced the room, meeting her gaze every few paces. "You've caused me no end of trouble. Now, Mary, here…she's been all right, until she saw you slung over my man's shoulders like a sack of flour. Then, she threatened to raise quite the ruckus."

Nina's heart warmed to think that timid Mary had come to her defense. "You can't keep us here forever. Eventually, the building will be searched either by the city to determine whether the structure is stable or by the authorities when they realize we're missing." Her comment might cause him to move her and Mary. At least she hoped so. If they were to be moved, they had a greater chance of being seen.

"Oh, you're a smart one." Barton wagged his finger in front of her face. "Let me tell you one thing, little missy. You won't be leaving this room for a very long time." He laughed and exited the same way he had come.

"Why are you trying to make him angry?" Mary's eyes widened. "You need to promise him you'll behave. Say you want to join him. Anything! He'll take your children when you're not looking, in exchange for that promise."

"I'll do no such thing." She couldn't conceive of making such promises. "I want him to leave us alone until we're either rescued or I come up with a plan."

"I've seen the way your plans work." Mary scowled, trying to pull her leg free of the chair. "I don't want any part of another one."

Nina wrinkled her nose and peered through the gloom. She would never let someone take her children in exchange for her stealing for them.

Boxes were stacked almost to the ceiling along one wall. A battered metal desk was pushed against another. A small boarded window was above the desk, allowing a bit of the setting sun to squeeze through the cracks in the board and paint the scuffed floor with strips of melon. The desk seemed to be her best bet.

She bounced up and down until the chair made slow progress across the room. If she could make it to the desk, maybe she could cut the rope around her hands on the corner.

"Stop it," Mary hissed. "You're making too much noise."

"They aren't listening too closely, I'll guess. We're tied up. What can we possibly get into?" Nina continued her rough ride across the floor.

Once she reached the desk, she flopped the chair around and felt for a sharp edge. Anything that would cut through the rope fibers. As Mary continued to toss out words of doom and gloom, Nina was tempted to ask her to gnaw through the rope just to get her to be quiet.

Oh, God, help us. There! A bit of metal stuck out from the side of the desk leg.

Nina scooted the chair closer and sawed away, biting her lip when the rope would slip and the metal scraped her flesh. Footsteps sounded outside the door. She quickly bounced a few feet from the desk and tried to look as innocent as possible.

Barton's right-hand man brought in a cup of water and two slices of bread. "Boss says I got to feed you." He upended the cup to Mary's mouth, then to Nina's before shoving pieces of the bread between their lips. He peered closer at Nina. "Weren't you over there?" He motioned his head.

"If I were over there, how would I have gotten over here?" She tilted her head, hoping the man was as dense as he appeared.

He was. He shrugged and left.

Nina heard a key turn in the lock. "I bet that means we won't be seeing any more of them tonight." She moved back to the desk and sawed slower than before, trying to spare her skin. By the time she had finished, the rope pieces falling to the floor with muffled thuds, Mary was snoring.

How could the woman be sleeping? Nina's hands might be free, but she and Mary weren't out of danger yet. The knots around her ankles were too tight to undo with her fingers. She rummaged through the drawers of the desk, finally finding a rusty pair of scissors. By the time she had cut through the ropes tying her ankles to the chair legs, perspiration dripped from her brow and ran between her shoulder blades. If they didn't get free soon, she'd catch a chill.

"Mary." Nina shook her.

She squirmed.

"Settle down. I don't want to cut you." Nina worked on her ropes. "I'm not sure how we can get out of here, but you're pretty small. Maybe you can squeeze through that window."

"And then what?"

"Go for help." Nina freed Mary's hands free and started working on her legs. "Maybe you can search the building for your daughter."

"Do you think she's here?"

Nina shrugged. "Why not? Here is as good a place as any."

Mary stood, threw off the last of her ropes and rushed to the window, with Nina right behind her. Together, they yanked against the wood and barely managed to pull it an inch from the wall.

"This isn't going to work." Mary's shoulders sagged.

"Need some help?"

Nina glanced up into the handsome, smiling face of Jacob. She covered her face with her hands, and cried. She didn't have to be strong alone. Jacob was there.

Jacob wanted nothing more than to put his arms around Nina and hold her close. But first, he had to get her out of there. He made hand signals for the other soldiers to skirt around the building, then pulled back and kicked the board off the window. It clattered to the floor.

Both women glanced at the door. When no one came to investigate the noise, they both scrambled onto the top of the desk. The window was too small for either of them.

"Wait there," Jacob said. "Away from the door. I'll find another way in."

Jacob scooted from the window, plastering his back against the wall. For the first time in almost fifteen years, he wasn't afraid. He'd learned through his studies that no power was greater than the One who was in him. Nina shared that same faith. They'd be all right.

"Sir!" A soldier peeked around the corner of the building. "We count four criminals inside. They all carry weapons. Want us to take them out?"

"Alive, if at all possible. Look for a little girl being held in a room other than the one the two women are in." He hoped the child was held in the same building. If not, she might be lost forever. Sold into slavery in Mexico. Put up for adoption in the east. He shook his head. For Mary's sake, he hoped they found the child unharmed.

Since the soldiers had refused to lend Jacob a weapon, because he was no longer a member of the armed forces, he stayed behind them as they burst through the front door. He spotted Johnny hiding in the shadows across the street and motioned for the boy to stay.

"Well, well, well." Barton stepped from a hall doorway and held a pistol to Jacob's head. "If it isn't the sergeant, and out of uniform, too."

Jacob stiffened. "Just give us the women and the girl, and you'll get out of this alive."

"I think I will be the one leaving on two legs."

Jacob whirled, slamming his shoulder into the man's stomach. The gun went off, sounding loud in the empty hallway. Two soldiers rushed back. Both of them held their weapons on Barton. Jacob struggled to his feet, wiping his hands on his pants.

"You were saying, Mr. Barton?"

The man cursed and spat at Jacob's feet before he was dragged outside. Soon, after a few more gunshots that, thankfully, missed their targets, the soldiers rounded up the rest of Barton's men. Jacob and a few soldiers unbolted the door barricading Nina and Mary inside.

"My baby?" Mary clutched his shirt.

"Not yet."

A woman screamed from somewhere down the hall. Jacob's gaze collided with Nina's.

"Go," she said. "I'll be here."

He raced toward the sound. If the soldiers had found the child, she might not be as frightened by a man out of uniform.

When he arrived at the farthest room, he saw that the soldiers had cornered a woman. On a cot under the window, sat a red-haired girl under the age of five. Jacob knelt in front of her. "Do you want to see your mommy?"

She nodded, sticking a dirty thumb in her mouth. He had no sooner picked her up, then Mary and Nina barged into the room. Mary immediately wrapped her child in her arms, leaving Jacob free to do the same with Nina.

She cried as he held her, tears dampening the front of his shirt. He rubbed her back, resting his cheek against the softness of her hair.

"I knew you'd come." She raised her tear-streaked face to his.

"Was there any doubt?" He would have faced the four men by himself in order to get her back. He rubbed his thumb across her cheeks, wiping away the tears. "I'm sorry I had to leave in the first place."

"My idea about the film didn't quite work out the way I'd planned."

Jacob laughed, and putting his arm around her shoulder, led her outside. The soldiers had already led Barton and his men to jail, leaving Jacob to escort the women back to their cottage.

"The police will have questions for both of you tomorrow."

Nina nodded. "I'll be glad to tell them what I know. It

isn't much. I gave some speeches at the camp common areas and was grabbed on my way home."

"Do I even want to know about these speeches?"

"No, Mr. Taft," Mary said. "You do not. That woman of yours is teched in the head."

Woman of his. He liked the sound of that. He took her hands in his, noticing the scrapes on her wrists. "You're injured."

"I'll be—"

"Miss Hansen!" Johnny raced across the street and wrapped his arms around Nina. "When I saw you in that room—"

"So it was you who cried the alarm. We owe you our lives."

He ducked his head. "Not really. Miss Agnes told Mr. Taft the moment he showed up at the cottage. I just knew the good buildings to hold people prisoner."

Jacob ruffled his hair. "If not for you, we might still be looking." He hoped Nina liked his plan for their future. He couldn't imagine spending the rest of his life away from her or the children she collected.

"Between you and Johnny," he said to Nina, "the city will never be the same."

"I hope not," Nina said. "The people might as well improve right along with the reconstruction of buildings." She patted her stomach. "I'm starving. All Barton gave us was a slice of bread."

"I think Agnes might have something to feed you, and we need to care for your wrists." He sent Johnny ahead to let Agnes know they were coming, then glanced to where Mary walked ahead of them, her child still in her arms. "Your cottage gets more full every time I see you."

Nina wrapped her arms around his waist. "Isn't it a blessing?"

"I never thought I'd say so, but yes, it is." He stopped in front of the gift he had bought for her. "I'm not sure if this is the right time or not, but what do you think of filling that house with children?"

She glanced from the house to him and back to the house. "This house is on my dream list." She sighed and leaned against the fence. "Isn't it grand? Hardly damaged at all by the fires. Nothing that a fresh coat of paint can't fix. Oh." She pointed at a sold sign. "It's just as well. I would never have been able to afford it by taking pictures."

Jacob stood behind her and turned her to face him. "I bought the house, Nina. I went to Kansas to settle my land, and wired the money here for the purchase. I ended up renting the land to a family friend. My military monthly pension will cover the mortgage on this house. So, what do you say? Shall we fill it with children? Especially that little Sally."

"What are you saying?"

"I'm saying." He got down on one knee and pulled his mother's ring from his pocket. "Will you marry me, Nina Hansen, tarnished ring and all?"

"Was this the ring your mother wore in the fire?" Tears shimmered in her eyes.

"Yes. It's all I have left of her."

Nina slipped it on her finger. "What could be more perfect than a ring that had survived a fire and a love that grew from one? Of course, I'll marry you. When?"

Jacob whooped and jumped to his feet, swinging her around. "As soon as possible, and we'll get a real preacher, no disrespect to Herbert."

Nina laughed and kissed him, sending his heart soaring to the stars.

Chapter 18

Nina got dressed in a tent Jacob had pitched on the sand. They were getting married on the beach in a few minutes, then spending their wedding night alone in the house he had bought. Tomorrow, the others would join them, all becoming part of the Taft Orphanage.

Neither of them cared that a brisk ocean breeze blew. This was their special place. Nowhere else would be as perfect for their wedding.

Agnes entered the tent. "You look beautiful."

Nina smoothed her hands down the light blue gown. "Where in the world did Herbert find such a beautiful dress?"

"He ordered it through his shop. Mine is yellow." Agnes smiled. "I can't believe I'll be marrying him in a week. Thank you for letting us live in the guest house in back of the orphanage."

Nina took her hands in hers. "Thank you for agreeing to stay on as a cook. It's the least I could do in exchange for all you've done, and will be doing."

"You're family." Agnes gave her a hug. "Word is spreading quickly about what you want to do about the city's lost children. Every room will be filled before you know it." She planted a kiss on Nina's cheek and left.

Nina nodded, intending to take a photograph of every

child needing a home and sending information to news-papers across the country. She turned back to the small mirror propped on a chest and tucked an errant strand of hair into its chignon. Her hands trembled.

For weeks, months, she had despaired that Jacob would ever find peace or see his worth. Now that he had, she would become his wife. Who was she to be so blessed?

"My dear, you look lovely."

Nina turned and gasped. "Mrs. Fox!" She threw herself in the other woman's arms. "How are you? The children?"

"We're all fine. Mr. Taft notified me of your marriage." She held Nina at arm's length. "I wouldn't miss this for the world. He also told me of your grand plans and hired me to help you. Do you have room for an old woman and five more children? The others have all found a home in another orphanage, and I came back for you. I'd love to work with you again."

Nina's heart squeezed. "Of course I do." She gazed upon the precious face of the woman who had raised her. "Since you are the only parent I can remember, will you do the honor of giving my hand in marriage?"

Mrs. Fox's eyes shimmered. "I can't think of anything I'd rather do. Now, don't you think it's time you started calling me Alice?"

"I think so. Seeing you makes my day more perfect."

"Then let's get you married. Your groom is waiting to see his beautiful bride. Oh, my dear, you're as pretty as the summer sunshine." Alice linked her arm with Nina's.

They stepped into a fall afternoon. Everyone that had lived under Nina's roof, and those she had helped since the quake, sat in borrowed chairs or stools, facing the ocean. Mrs. Stoltz turned and beamed. Herbert stood at Jacob's side, Agnes across from them. Everyone they loved had come to celebrate the day.

Nina's gaze locked with Jacob's, not swerving during the long stroll she took down the aisle. She was getting married! Alice placed Nina's hand into Jacob's before taking her own seat.

"Dearly beloved." The pastor, whose credentials had been personally checked by Jacob, beamed across the crowd. "We are gathered here today..."

Nina hardly heard the words spoken by the pastor, so intently did she focus on Jacob, resplendent in a dark gray suit. Laughter rang out when she didn't respond to her cue of saying "I do." Face heating, Nina repeated her vows.

"You may now kiss your bride."

Jacob pulled her to him, dipped her over his arm and planted a kiss on her that made everything around them evaporate. She wrapped her arms around his neck and kissed him back, showing all her love for him in that moment. When he straightened and took her hand, he whispered, "I love you."

"Family and friends," the pastor said, his voice booming across the sand, "I present to you, Mr. and Mrs. Jacob Taft."

* * * * *

Dear Reader,

The 1906 San Francisco earthquake was a momentous disaster, yet the human spirit prevailed. While some of my dates might be off as to when certain things became available for the survivors, I did my best to be as accurate as possible, and to show how love can grow during even the most dire circumstances.

Throughout history, mankind has proven to have an insurmountable strength and will to prevail. I hope you witness this during this series of love stories of which this is the first, and enjoy these sweet stories of romance and faith.

I'd love to hear from you. Please visit me at www.cynthiahickey.com.

God bless you,
Cynthia Hickey

REQUEST YOUR FREE BOOKS!

2 FREE INSPIRATIONAL NOVELS
PLUS 2
FREE
MYSTERY GIFTS

Love Inspired

YES! Please send me 2 FREE Love Inspired® novels and my 2 FREE mystery gifts (gifts are worth about $10). After receiving them, if I don't wish to receive any more books, I can return the shipping statement marked "cancel." If I don't cancel, I will receive 6 brand-new novels every month and be billed just $4.74 per book in the U.S. or $5.24 per book in Canada. That's a savings of at least 21% off the cover price. It's quite a bargain! Shipping and handling is just 50¢ per book in the U.S. and 75¢ per book in Canada.* I understand that accepting the 2 free books and gifts places me under no obligation to buy anything. I can always return a shipment and cancel at any time. Even if I never buy another book, the two free books and gifts are mine to keep forever.

105/305 IDN F49N

Name _____ (PLEASE PRINT) _____

Address _____ Apt. #

City _____ State/Prov. _____ Zip/Postal Code

Signature (if under 18, a parent or guardian must sign) _____

Mail to the **Harlequin® Reader Service:**
IN U.S.A.: P.O. Box 1867, Buffalo, NY 14240-1867
IN CANADA: P.O. Box 609, Fort Erie, Ontario L2A 5X3

Are you a subscriber to Love Inspired books
and want to receive the larger-print edition?
Call 1-800-873-8635 or visit www.ReaderService.com.

* Terms and prices subject to change without notice. Prices do not include applicable taxes. Sales tax applicable in N.Y. Canadian residents will be charged applicable taxes. Offer not valid in Quebec. This offer is limited to one order per household. Not valid for current subscribers to Love Inspired books. All orders subject to credit approval. Credit or debit balances in a customer's account(s) may be offset by any other outstanding balance owed by or to the customer. Please allow 4 to 6 weeks for delivery. Offer available while quantities last.

Your Privacy—The Harlequin® Reader Service is committed to protecting your privacy. Our Privacy Policy is available online at www.ReaderService.com or upon request from the Harlequin Reader Service.
We make a portion of our mailing list available to reputable third parties that offer products we believe may interest you. If you prefer that we not exchange your name with third parties, or if you wish to clarify or modify your communication preferences, please visit us at www.ReaderService.com/consumerschoice or write to us at Harlequin Reader Service Preference Service, P.O. Box 9062, Buffalo, NY 14269. Include your complete name and address.

LIDIR13R

REQUEST YOUR FREE BOOKS!

2 FREE INSPIRATIONAL NOVELS
PLUS 2
FREE
MYSTERY GIFTS

Love Inspired
HISTORICAL
INSPIRATIONAL HISTORICAL ROMANCE

YES! Please send me 2 FREE Love Inspired® Historical novels and my 2 FREE mystery gifts (gifts are worth about $10). After receiving them, if I don't wish to receive any more books, I can return the shipping statement marked "cancel." If I don't cancel, I will receive 4 brand-new novels every month and be billed just $4.74 per book in the U.S. or $5.24 per book in Canada. That's a savings of at least 21% off the cover price. It's quite a bargain! Shipping and handling is just 50¢ per book in the U.S. and 75¢ per book in Canada.* I understand that accepting the 2 free books and gifts places me under no obligation to buy anything. I can always return a shipment and cancel at any time. Even if I never buy another book, the two free books and gifts are mine to keep forever.

102/302 IDN F5CY

Name	(PLEASE PRINT)	
Address		Apt. #
City	State/Prov.	Zip/Postal Code

Signature (if under 18, a parent or guardian must sign)

Mail to the **Harlequin® Reader Service:**
IN U.S.A.: P.O. Box 1867, Buffalo, NY 14240-1867
IN CANADA: P.O. Box 609, Fort Erie, Ontario L2A 5X3

Want to try two free books from another series?
Call 1-800-873-8635 or visit www.ReaderService.com.

* Terms and prices subject to change without notice. Prices do not include applicable taxes. Sales tax applicable in N.Y. Canadian residents will be charged applicable taxes. Offer not valid in Quebec. This offer is limited to one order per household. Not valid for current subscribers to Love Inspired Historical books. All orders subject to credit approval. Credit or debit balances in a customer's account(s) may be offset by any other outstanding balance owed by or to the customer. Please allow 4 to 6 weeks for delivery. Offer available while quantities last.

Your Privacy—The Harlequin® Reader Service is committed to protecting your privacy. Our Privacy Policy is available online at www.ReaderService.com or upon request from the Harlequin Reader Service.

We make a portion of our mailing list available to reputable third parties that offer products we believe may interest you. If you prefer that we not exchange your name with third parties, or if you wish to clarify or modify your communication preferences, please visit us at www.ReaderService.com/consumerschoice or write to us at Harlequin Reader Service Preference Service, P.O. Box 9062, Buffalo, NY 14269. Include your complete name and address.

LIHDIR13R

ReaderService.com

Manage your account online!

- Review your order history
- Manage your payments
- Update your address

> *We've designed*
> *the Harlequin® Reader Service*
> *website just for you.*

Enjoy all the features!

- Reader excerpts from any series
- Respond to mailings and
  special monthly offers
- Discover new series available to you
- Browse the Bonus Bucks catalog
- Share your feedback

Visit us at:
ReaderService.com